Deadly Reunion

JEFFREY ASHFORD

Deadly Reunion

St. Martin's Press
New York

Library of Congress Cataloging-in-Publication Data

Ashford, Jeffrey
    Deadly reunion / Jeffrey Ashford.
        p.   cm.
    ISBN·0-312-07695-9
    I. Title.
    PR6060.E43D44   1992
    823'.914—dc20   92-1073
                                                                   CIP

First published in Great Britain by HarperCollins Publishers.

First U.S. Edition: May 1992
10 9 8 7 6 5 4 3 2 1

CHAPTER 1

Gary Weston's thoughts, rather at odds with the brilliant sunshine, were interrupted by a bellow from behind. 'By God, if it isn't old Aggie!'

He turned to find himself face to face with a man whose most noticeable feature was a ginger beard of triffid luxuriance. The nickname 'Aggie' was specific to his schooldays and he struggled to link this man with one of the boys he'd known then. Curly hair, a shade redder than the beard, a deep forehead, very blue eyes, a Roman nose, and lurking within the beard a pair of sensuous lips; solidly built and clear signs of a belly; a contempt for neat appearance—both T-shirt and shorts were creased and could have been cleaner. He could recall only three redheads, one of whom had ever been contemptuous of standards. 'Jason?' He remembered the nickname. 'Windy?'

'Took you bloody long enough!' Farley pulled out one of the free chairs and sat, careless that he was outside the shade of the sun umbrella which was set through the centre of the table. He said mockingly: 'Or were you hoping that if you made out you couldn't remember me, I'd clear off?'

'It took time to penetrate the whiskers.'

'Still the diplomat.' He looked round for a waiter, saw one who had just crossed the road to the tables set out on the beach side, and called out in Spanish. The waiter, who'd been about to serve one of the other tables, hurried across.

'What are you drinking?' Farley asked.

'Gin and tonic. But I don't think I'll have another, thanks.'

'A wimpish thought.' He spoke to the waiter, who left.

'You know something? I can still remember your look of calculating distaste when I told you I'd been expelled. Working out how quickly you could distance yourself from trouble.'

'Wrong as ever,' replied Weston, with amusement. 'As far as I can remember now, I was wondering if there was any way in which I could help you.'

'Did I say I needed any help?'

'No, but only because you thought that that would be a sign of weakness.'

'You still don't understand! You've no idea why I took Madge into her father's day study instead of using the sports pavilion?'

'That's right, I don't. It was totally crazy and really asking for trouble.'

'I did it because two days before he'd bored us silly in hall with his warning against the evils of lust. What did that sanctimonious, dried-up hypocrite know about the joys of lust?' He laughed boisterously. 'And if his daughter hadn't enjoyed herself so much she gave tongue, he'd never have discovered us. I often wondered if afterwards she explained what he'd been missing.'

'Since she was his daughter, it can't have been quite as much as you think.'

'Her conception could only have been pursued in a spirit of dull duty.'

The waiter returned and put two glasses down on the table. Farley said something that raised a temporary smile on the waiter's tired, sweating face as he stuck a square of paper on a spiked holder. As he hurried off, Farley moved the holder to read the bill. 'Bloody robbers. You can buy a whole litre of reasonable gin for what they're charging for two drinks. It's no wonder the bar owners drive around in Porsches.'

On the beach, a young, shapely woman, wearing the

bottom half of a bikini, stood; unhurriedly, she put on the top half. She rolled up the mat on which she'd been lying, collected up towel and purse, and walked on to the pavement and across the road to a hotel. Farley, who'd been watching her, turned back and drank. 'So what's your CV say? Married, two kids, a mortgaged house in suburbia, and your one ambition to live long enough to draw a pension?'

'Your idea of absolute hell?'

'Add in a mother-in-law with Alzheimer's and you're right.'

'I've a mother-in-law, but she's far from senile.' Just malicious, he could have added.

'Stockbroker, Lloyd's, assistant manager with NatWest?'

'Public relations.'

'Wouldn't have said you were a good enough liar for that.'

'You could well be right. I've just been made redundant.'

'You're unemployed?'

'I find the expression "resting" more soothing to the ego.'

'So where's the lady wife? Resting in the hotel?'

'Back at home.'

'You've been allowed an extra-marital ration of sun, sea, and sex?'

'At the last moment she couldn't come.'

'You always were a lucky bastard.'

'Fortune favours the bold; luck favours the worthy.'

Farley laughed. 'I hope you've put the kids down for St Brede's and are teaching them the school songs; bowdlerized versions, naturally?'

'We've no children.'

'She'd rather read a book?'

'Because one or other of us is probably infertile,' replied Weston, hiding his distaste for so personal a question.

Farley abruptly changed the subject. 'D'you remember that little slime, Tipples?'

Every one of them had had a nickname, some cruel enough to have made their bearers' lives miserable. Weston thought back and eventually identified a small, nervous, perpetually homesick boy who had been more afraid of Farley's extrovert buffoonery than the occasional sadistic attention of the form bully. 'I can just about place him.'

'I was in the UK a couple of years back and banged into him in Mincing Lane. Silly little sod tried to make out he hadn't a clue who I was.' Farley drained his glass, turned round and saw the waiter who'd previously served him. He waved and the waiter threaded his way between the tables, obeying the summons even though that meant he ignored a similar call from someone nearer.

'No more for me,' said Weston.

Farley spoke rapidly to the waiter, then, as the latter left, said: 'When were you last gloriously tight?'

'Some time ago and it wasn't glorious.'

'Miserable as ever!' Farley spoke as if he gained some satisfaction from that observation. 'So how are you spending your miserable time in Restina?'

'Doing what comes naturally. Swimming, sunbathing, eating too much, drinking sensibly, and sleeping the sleep of the just.'

'No women?'

'It is possible to live without them.'

'It's possible to live on goat's milk and bananas, but who the hell wants to? Have you been to El Diablo yet?'

'I don't think so. What and where is it?'

'A nightclub with a floor show you won't see in Surbiton. I'll take you there. Or does your conventional soul shudder at the thought of the unconventional?'

'My middle name's tolerance.' It was annoying to find himself trying to avert Farley's scorn, just as he had done when a schoolboy.

The waiter returned and put down two glasses, collected up Farley's empty one, spiked the second bill.

Farley drank. 'D'you still sail?'

'Not recently; there just hasn't been the time.' At school, they'd both been very keen sailors and had made a good team. Farley had been aggressive, he had been cautious, and this had been a useful combination for a 420 sailed on a lake which was surrounded by hills which funnelled the wind to make it erratic. They had won the inter-house competition two years in succession. 'What about you?'

'I still do a bit now and then,' replied Farley with studied vagueness. He drained his glass. 'Where are you staying?'

'At the Bahia Azul.'

'Your Spanish sounds like an Englishman trying to speak Swedish. I'll be in touch and we'll go to El Diablo. Give you something to talk to your wife about.' He stood. 'I'll see the waiter, so don't let him rip you off.' He pulled the slips of paper off the spike. 'They're all bloody Andaluce gipsies and will screw a blind man if he's not looking.'

'One round's my shout.'

'You're unemployed—remember.'

A kind gesture, clumsily made, or a contemptuous gesture, crudely made? Weston couldn't decide. Any more than he could decide whether or not the unexpected meeting had been welcome.

He crossed the hotel bedroom, sat on the left-hand bed, picked up the telephone receiver, and asked the receptionist to get his home number. The connection was soon made. 'Hullo, darling, how are things?'

Stephanie, showing no signs of being glad to hear from him, replied that things had been difficult. Her mother had not been feeling very well and had rung the surgery and told the receptionist to tell the doctor to visit her. The receptionist had refused to do so unless she knew what the trouble was so that she could judge its urgency. Her mother had put the insolent woman in her place. The doctor had told her that he couldn't spare the time for a home visit unless she were seriously ill, which it did not sound as if she were . . .

His sympathies were all with the GP, but he tried to pour oil on the troubled waters. 'I'm afraid doctors have to be reluctant to make a home visit . . .'

She interrupted him to express, at length, her opinion of doctors who treated their patients as mere ciphers and couldn't distinguish the wheat from the chaff. She did not ask him how he was or whether he was enjoying the holiday, nor did she respond when he said—perhaps a shade duti-fully—that he was missing her. He said goodbye.

The drinks in the hotel bar were expensive, so he'd bought a bottle of gin and three of tonic at a nearby super-market and a pack of ice from a petrol station. He poured himself a generous drink, went out on to the balcony and sat on the cane chair there.

He drank and admitted to himself that the meeting with Farley had unsettled him. Or perhaps it was more accurate to say that the thoughts which the meeting had occasioned were unsettling. Had his life really become as bland as Farley had suggested? Did one have to challenge life in order to live it to the full? Was conformity necessarily the mark of insignificance?

He stared out at the sea, dark and formless except where the thin moonlight washed across it. The red port light of a late-returning yacht, making for her berth, moved slowly. He'd always hoped to sail regularly after leaving school and when he'd still allowed himself daydreams, he'd crewed the winning 12-metre in the America's Cup . . . Daydreams were not solely the prerogative of youth. At his pre-wedding stag party, when enjoying that pleasant midway state between not sober, not drunk, he had assured himself that from the next day on Stephanie would cease to need or welcome so emotionally close a relationship with her mother ... The cynics said that marriage was a lottery from which the winning number had been withdrawn. His own marriage had first turned sour when he'd tried to make Stephanie accept that her relationship with her mother could not take precedence over her relationship with him ...

He finished his drink, went back into the bedroom to pour out another. Jason Farley would at least have approved of that.

CHAPTER 2

Thirty-five years before, Restina had been a very small fishing port on the Costa del Sol which still lived in the past. Relatively inaccessible, it could be approached only by a single track which was occasionally washed away when there was heavy rain in the mountains and the torrente filled and overflowed. The only foreigners who'd visited it had been young men with beards and women with straggly hair who backpacked, were searching for the meaning of life, had little or no money and extolled the virtues of poverty. The villagers, who knew all about poverty, had thought them mad and therefore treated them with forbearance.

Then a developer had ventured down the single track in a Land-Rover. He'd climbed out and looked at the rough, simple stone homes—one had green shutters and in this had lived an accommodating widow—the only bar, the only shop, the poster-blue sea and the battered fishing-boats drawn up on the beach of virgin sand, and he had seen hotels, appartments, restaurants, cafés, shops, ice-cream parlours, discothèques . . .

Thirty-five years later, Restina was a brash holiday resort known to hundreds of thousands; the developer was a multi-millionaire, all of whose black money was safely out of the country; and the villagers, cheated, bewildered, stripped of their own standards, had become unwanted refugees who could not understand why their children denied their authority and laughed at them for being unable to read or write—even the accommodating widow (or rather her successor) found that few were stupid enough to pay her the few pesetas she asked when young and beautiful foreigners charged nothing.

José Muñoz stared through the window of the bar and watched Miguel climb into the Escort cabriolet and drive off. He drained his glass, put it down on the bar. The barman, a surly Galician, picked up a bottle of brandy and prepared to pour. 'No more,' Muñoz said.

'Then it's a hundred and thirty.' The Galician was a man of as few words as possible.

'A hundred and thirty for two coñacs? Have you started charging tourist prices, you poxy robber?'

The Galician was unmoved by insults.

'Put it down on a chit.'

He pulled open a drawer and brought out several small and uneven bundles of paper, each held together with a paperclip. He found the one he wanted, wrote on the top sheet. 'It's a thousand and fifteen. On Saturday.'

'All right, all right. I'll bloody well pay you on Saturday or you'll have a heart attack.'

One of the other men present said: 'Don't, and give us all good reason for a laugh.'

Muñoz left and walked along the pavement towards the front, passing shops which sold trashy tourist mementoes, cafés, bars, and a couple of restaurants. He jingled the coins in his right-hand pocket. Miguel had driven off to Ronda to see his maiden aunt who was dying; a journey made not from love but because the old cow owned several properties which were worth many millions of pesetas. So now he was free to seek out the blonde Norwegian who never missed a chance of displaying her luscious body, shapely enough to bring life back to a septuagenarian.

Miguel Bartret had gone not to Ronda—word had come through that his aunt had rallied—but to Oreda, the nearest town. He returned to Restina at 11.15 and drove into one of the front car parks, left the car and walked along the cobbled path which bordered the beach for half a kilometre. When half way, he turned off on to the sand and searched among the sunbathers for Märthe. He failed to find her. He spoke to the man who hired out pedalos who said, not without a touch of malicious amusement, that Märthe had been on the beach earlier, but that she'd then left with a man.

'Who?' demanded Bartret furiously.

'José. Didn't you know?'

He swore with passion. His best friend, José; a gipsy bastard who'd been eyeing Märthe like a dog after a bitch on heat . . .

He drove home. There, he collected his largest hunting knife. When his mother saw him with this in his hands, he said he was searching for a piece of mierda and when he found him, he'd cut off his cojones. She wanted to tell him not to do anything so dangerous, but was far too proud a mother actually to speak such cowardly words. Deprive a man of his honour and one deprived him of the reason to live.

He visited everywhere it was reasonable to expect Märthe and José to be, without success, then remembered that she'd often asked him to drive her up Puig Leone to see the view from the crest. He'd never taken her because it was an absurd waste of time. But a condón like José might indulge her stupid fancy in order to earn her compliance.

On the main coastal road he could drive recklessly and at speed. Once he turned off that on to the narrow, arrow-straight road, he could drive recklessly and at very great speed. Even up the winding mountain road, he remained dangerous.

The lookout point, some two hundred metres below the crest of Puig Leone, had been levelled and enlarged until it could accommodate a couple of tourist buses and a dozen cars. There were no buses present and only three other cars, but one of these was José's battered green Ibiza. Visible were one couple and a group of four, but not the two he was after. The treacherous bastard had taken her off somewhere where he could assail her innocence. Since the only way they could have gone, unless they were experienced rock-climbers, was along a ridge to the left which led to a belt of pine trees which inexplicably grew in splendid isolation, Miguel climbed over the guard rail and on to that ridge.

He found them beyond the trees, in the shade of an outcrop of rock. José was clearly more embarrassed than Märthe since absurdly he grabbed his shirt and held it in front of himself while she just watched, a quiet smile on her beautiful lips. Miguel drew his knife and, to the accompaniment of wild threats, raced forward. His right foot caught in a fissure and sent him sprawling; his head struck a rock and he was knocked unconscious.

Farley walked into Bar Español and spoke to the surly Galician. 'I'm looking for Miguel Bartret. I've been along to his home, but he wasn't in and neither was his mother. Have you any idea where I'll find him?'

Had another foreigner come into the bar and asked after Bartret, the Galician would either not have answered or would have denied knowing him. But Farley's flamboyant, friendly manner drew a response even from a man from Galicia. 'She's looking after him in the hospital.'

'What's happened?'

'He's got a broken skull,' said one of the other men present.

'That's bloody bad luck.'

'Bloody good luck for José.' There was laughter.

Farley suggested everyone had a drink and when these had been served, brought out a packet of cheroots. He wondered what had happened to poor Miguel. They told him, even the Galician adding a ribald comment.

He left the café and walked down to the front and along to the wooden building which housed a telephone exchange for tourists, which operated during the season. He checked the number of the state hospital in Ronda, asked the woman behind the counter to get it for him. In less than a minute she waved him into one of the booths.

It was customary in Spain when asked for information to deny any knowledge about anything, even if it were one's job to give such information. But by using all his charm, Farley was able to persuade the woman in the hospital to whom he spoke to find out what she could about Miguel Bartret's condition.

She told him that Bartret had suffered a fractured skull and although it was not thought he had suffered any damage to his brain, nevertheless it would be a few days before the doctors would be certain and he could be discharged.

Farley paid for the call, left the exchange, and walked along to a stall where he bought a pistachio ice-cream. As he ate, he stared at the boats which were tied up against the western arm of the harbour and silently cursed Miguel with Spanish imagination and English crudeness. Two days to go and now no crew. What the hell did he do? Sail on his own? That would be possible, but foolhardy. And while it might seem to others that he treated life carelessly, he was never foolhardy at sea. So he had to find another crewman. There were still a dozen fishing-boats which worked from the harbour and any one of the fishermen would be an efficient crew member, but how to be sure he did not have a loose mouth? Miguel had had to keep his mouth shut; he'd no such hold on any of the other fishermen . . .

He watched a ketch under power come astern from her berth and then turn to line up for the harbour entrance. A young, leggy woman was preparing the spinnaker for hoisting and he criticized her every move because he was a traditionalist and held that sailing boats and women did not mix . . . For some reason, the sight of that woman triggered a suggestion in his mind. He lit a cheroot and smoked as he examined the idea. Initially, it seemed an absurd one. By definition, an honest man would not knowingly engage in a dishonest enterprise; if tricked into doing so, he would report the fact to the authorities as soon as possible. But while an honest man's sense of honesty might be invariable, his reactions to dishonesty might well not be if he had been conditioned by the past and in him there had been bred a loyalty even stronger than that which he gave to his concept of honesty . . .

At St Brede's, as at any school, there had been a score of unwritten rules for every new boy to learn and observe. Of these, one had been of paramount importance. Thou shalt not rat on thy fellows. Even if one were being bullied unmercifully, one did not admit the fact to anyone in authority. The loyalty one owed one's companions was absolute. Gary Weston was the kind of naïve idealist who'd continue to observe loyalties long after life should have taught him that it was profitable only to observe them towards oneself.

CHAPTER 3

Weston was sitting on the balcony of his hotel bedroom when the telephone rang. It abruptly reminded him that he should have phoned Stephanie earlier. A duty delayed was a duty betrayed. He put the glass down, hurried into the bedroom, sat on the nearer bed and lifted the receiver. 'Hullo, darling. I've been trying to ring you, but couldn't get through.'

A man said, lisping heavily: 'I've nearly died from disappointment,'

'Who . . . Who's that?'

There was a bellow of raucous laughter.

'Jason? . . . Sorry about the greeting, but I thought you were Stephanie.'

'I'll believe you this time. Come on down, we're off for a meal.' He cut the connection.

Weston went back to the balcony, picked up the glass and finished the drink. It was typical of Farley not to bother to ask him if he'd like to go out for dinner.

Farley, wearing a brightly coloured shirt, grey linen trousers which were too tight about the waist, and sandals, was chatting to the receptionist, who was smiling. He made one last comment, which caused the receptionist to laugh out loud, then crossed the foyer. 'We'll try Casa Pepe.'

A battered Renault 18 shooting-brake was parked immediately outside the hotel, on a solid yellow line. 'Doesn't look much, but she goes.' Farley slapped his hand down on the roof, much as he would have slapped a favourite horse's haunch. 'It's no good running anything decent out here. The mechanics don't know the difference between a spark plug and a crankshaft and on the roads it's dodgem cars all the way.'

He pulled out from the pavement immediately in front of an oncoming taxi. It seemed, thought Weston, who had braced himself for a collision, that Farley observed local customs.

They drove along the front road as far as a belt of pine trees which marked the western end of Restina, then turned inland. 'You can never guarantee the grub in any of the local restaurants,' said Farley, 'but Casa Pepe's usually reasonable. At least the choice isn't restricted to eggs and chips or Anglicized paella, which is all you get in Restina.'

'The hotel food is quite reasonable,' observed Weston.

'Never complain, never explain, and never bash the sergeant in public, eh?'

That had been the unofficial motto of members of St Brede's cadet force. (Official motto: *Ad unum omnes.*) It had carried its own meaning for smutty-minded schoolboys.

'D'you remember Choppy?' continued Farley.

Weston thought back. 'Choppy Armitage?'

'That day he got really pissed off and told the Major where to go and what to do when he got there . . .'

Farley continued to reminisce. Weston had forgotten many of the incidents and it needed considerable effort on his part to recall them. He was suprised that Farley should be so nostalgic because it seemed out of character.

A few kilometres further on they turned back towards the coast. The restaurant was halfway up a pine-covered hill which overlooked a bay. It had an outside patio and most of the tables on this were occupied and a superior head waiter informed them in broken English that the remaining ones were reserved and they would have to eat inside. Farley exerted his charm and the head waiter agreed that perhaps one of the tables could be unreserved.

They sat. A waitress handed each of them a menu,

printed in Spanish, English, German, and French, and a
waiter put down a saucer of olives and a plate of thickly
cut bread and offered them the wine list. Without bothering
to consult it, Farley ordered a bottle of Codorníu Extra
Brut and Torres Sangre de Toro.

'The olives are locally cured and something of an
acquired taste,' he said. 'It helps if you like peppery arnica.'

Weston tried one. It was sufficiently bitter to convince
him that it was a taste he was unlikely to acquire.

Farley briefly studied the menu. 'The gazpacho's made
from a recipe of the Andalusian Moors and is good; I can
recommend the lomo con col—that is, provided you're not
totally suburban in your tastes.'

'I'm sufficiently suburban to want to know what it is
before I settle for it.'

'Loin of pork wrapped in cabbage leaves with sobra-
sada—which is a kind of raw sausage from the Balearics—
pine kernels, raisins, and anything left over from the night
before.'

'You make it sound pure ambrosia.'

Farley grinned, looked round. 'Where the hell's the
bubbly got to?'

Weston stared out at the bay which lay below them. The
sun was low and would soon dip below the western hills;
away from its glare, the sky held the mauve tinge which
came from great heat; the sea was a travel-poster blue; a
couple of yachts, their multicoloured sails barely filled, were
making for the marina at the eastern end of the bay, while
closer inshore, power boats were creaming the water, tow-
ing skiers. A scene that the London office worker dreamt
about on a raw, drizzling, January day.

The waiter brought the champagne in a wine cooler
together with two flutes. He opened the bottle, filled their
glasses, wished them good drinking.

Farley raised his glass. 'F.T.L.O.T.'

When they'd smuggled into school a few cans of beer and were about to drink them surreptitiously, that had been their toast. They'd been irrationally proud of the fact that the last three letters, which stood for Lot Of Them, had repeated part of their meaning . . . It had, thought Weston, been Farley who had composed their toast, just as it had been Farley who had promoted such sessions. He had had continually to challenge authority.

'It's not vintage Dom Perignon,' said Farley, 'but it's not bad.'

'It's popular at home for serving after the second glassful of the genuine.'

'With the label discreetly hidden by a napkin?'

'Of course.'

'You approve?'

'Why not? Especially if I'm paying the bill.'

'You can live with hypocrisy? That surprises me. I'd have placed you as one of the rare beings with the courage, or stupidity, always to tell the truth . . . But then, of course, that is to overlook your career in PR work.'

'It's also forgetting the fact that right now I have no such career.'

'I always was a tactless bastard.' He lifted the bottle out of the cooler and refilled their glasses.

'Don't look to me to disagree.'

Farley grinned. 'Sure.' He became serious. 'I suppose things are becoming rather tight for you financially?'

Weston disliked so personal a question. 'Not really.' He thought it probable that Farley would disbelieve him, imagining he was trying to retain some self-respect, but in a sense his answer was perfectly correct. Stephanie was wealthy and she'd never let the outside world have cause to think they were hard up.

Farley produced a pack of cheroots. 'D'you use these?'

'I don't, thanks.'

'Still as healthy in body as mind?'

'These days I can't run a hundred yards without puffing; probably my mind's in the same condition.'

Farley, cradling a balloon glass in the palm of his right hand, said: 'I'm sailing very soon on a short trip.'

'Where to?' Weston asked.

'Anywhere my fancy takes me.'

'What kind of yacht have you?'

'Not mine, but borrowed, so she's not a Camper and Nicholsons forty-five-foot ketch, but a sixty-foot Alder and Farson.'

'If you have to go power, you might as well do it in Rolls style.'

'I suppose so. And one thing, she's seaworthy enough in a bit of a sea. And plenty of luxury if that's what you're after. Beds, not bunks, showers, lavatories that don't drench you when you turn the wrong cock, every electronic navigational gadget that's been invented, a refrigerator that'll hold a dozen bottles of bubbly, a deep freeze, and a microwave to cook the convenience food and abolish slavery in the galley.'

'It sounds like the Ritz.'

'Take along a companion and it offers more than the Ritz, which can get absurdly stuffy about two sleeping in a room booked for one . . . I've been thinking.' He drained his glass. 'Why don't you come along? Give you the chance to escape the package holidaymakers and their snotty kids.'

'It sounds great, only . . .'

Farley interrupted him. 'And when it comes to the supercargo, what's your preference—blonde, brunette, or redhead?'

'You're forgetting I'm a married man.'

'That starts you off with two brownie points for experience.'

Weston shook his head. 'I'm rather old-fashioned about that sort of thing.'

'You sound as if you're bloody fossilized. But if that's the way you are, get your kicks from Mother Nature. We'll set sail on Tuesday at ten hundred hours.'

'I can't.'

'Why not? Are you frightened Mother Nature might seduce your soul?'

'I fly back on Tuesday.'

'You what? I thought you said you'd only arrived last Tuesday?'

'That's right. But I came out for just a week.'

Farley tugged at his beard, went to speak but checked the words, then looked round for the wine waiter and shouted a request for two more brandies. He lit a fresh cheroot. 'Tell you what. Come along and I'll fix up a fresh ticket home for you.'

'Sorry.'

'Are you scared you'll find someone else in your side of the bed if you stay away longer?'

Weston had forgotten how insultingly crude Farley could be if he did not get his own way. He was a born leader whose greatest fault was that he demanded that those who followed should do so unquestioningly.

The wine waiter brought over a bottle of Carlos I and refilled their glasses. Farley stared out at the bay, now in full darkness so that the shoreline was marked only by lights. His annoyance was obvious.

CHAPTER 4

After dinner on Monday night, Weston was sitting on the balcony of his bedroom and thinking the kind of thoughts which followed three-quarters of a bottle of Bach and a generous measure of Soberano when the phone rang. He was not to be caught out twice. 'Weston speaking.'

'It's your last night so we're off to El Diablo,' Farley said.

'What's that?'

'The nightclub I told you about. Pick you up in a quarter of an hour.' He cut the connection.

Weston wondered if he should refuse to go, to show Farley that he couldn't dictate the course of another's life. But wouldn't that be seen as no more than a petty, suburban gesture, worthy of mocking laughter?

Since this was Spain, it was three-quarters of an hour before Farley arrived at the hotel. He was not on his own. 'Jemma and Marcia,' he said, not bothering to identify who was who.

They were both tall, bean-pole thin, and long-legged; the one with curly black hair had dark brown eyes, a slightly upturned tip to her nose, and a laughing mouth; the one with wavy blonde hair had blue eyes, a straight nose, and generous, moist lips; both wore shirts, jeans and sandals; both had an easy, totally casual manner.

The Renault was again parked on a solid yellow line. Weston and the blonde were directed into the back seat and during the course of a five-minute drive he learned that he was with Jemma.

They parked by the side of a large, ugly, slab-sided building; that the illuminated name above the entrance lacked two letters added to the suggestion of tackiness, a suggestion further enhanced by the bare foyer and the short, dimly lit passage beyond. It was only when one passed through swing doors into the nightclub itself that one realized how a drab exterior had been used to heighten the visual impact of the interior.

The available space had been divided into two parts.

The larger, by far, contained tables and a dance floor; the smaller, a semi-circular stage. A tableau had been mounted, depicting the court of Diana or the Greek Artemis. (Later, it was to become clear that the presenter had either an ignorance of classical myths or a well-developed sense of irony.) The backdrop showed a scene of the chase; real and mythical beasts were hunted by godlike men. In the centre of the stage was a golden dais with a golden throne on it, initially unoccupied. Maidens, wearing many-pleated draperies, one breast bared, walked Afghans on golden leashes.

Farley's party was shown to one of the front tables by a waitress who wore a blouse with a neckline which plunged almost out of sight, a skirt too short to conceal, and black silk stockings with suspenders. Her bored, sulky expression briefly changed for the better when Farley ordered two bottles of champagne.

Their glasses filled, they drank. The glasses were refilled, the music restarted. Jemma spoke to Weston, but he had to shake his head to show that the surrounding noise was too great for him to understand her. She leant sideways so that her mouth was only inches away from his ear and suggested they dance; he was very conscious of the softness of her breast against his upper arm. 'I'm not much good at it.'

She straightened up, stood, took hold of his hand and pulled him to his feet. The dance floor was packed, but even allowing for that she snuggled up to him far more closely than was necessary. Automatically, and absurdly, he tried to move away. Her reaction was to draw even closer so that as they danced their legs were frequently entwined.

The music stopped and the dancers returned to their tables. There was a roll of drums, the lights dimmed. The maidens on the stage led their Afghans through a vine-draped gateway to go out of sight. When they returned without their dogs, Diana was in their midst. She was strikingly beautiful in a Nordic style and wore a long drapery, shot with gold thread, that was diaphanous; in her right hand, she held a bow. The maidens led her to the dais and helped her up on to it. She stood by the side of her throne, bow ready to draw and launch an arrow at her quarry. But there was none. Disappointed, she settled on the throne; bored, she closed her eyes. The maidens talked excitedly among themselves, then hurried off stage. They returned with a youth dressed in a tattered goatskin, and pointed at the throne. He stared at Diana with awe and fear and sank to his knees, gaze averted. The maidens called out and Diana opened her eyes, saw the youth, stood, raised and drew her bow, launched an invisible arrow. The youth cried out. Slowly, he came to his feet; like a sleepwalker, he approached the throne.

Weston emptied his glass. The performance was slick enough, but hopelessly dated; the kind of production one could have seen in a London nightclub forty years before. Farley reached across the table to refill his glass, winked. Jemma took the glass out of his hand, drank half the contents, handed it back, carefully making certain the marks of lipstick faced him.

On stage, Diana stepped down from the dais, approached the youth, leaned over to brush his curly hair with her lips. When he did not respond, she angrily motioned to the maidens. Two came forward, took hold of the goatskin and raised it over his head. He was naked. Diana ran her fingers down his cheeks, his neck, along his shoulders, down his chest . . .

Weston realized how naïve he'd been in comparing this act with any that had ever been shown in London. Embarrassed to be in the company of Jemma and Marcia, silently cursing Farley for bringing them along, he turned to Jemma to suggest they left before the inevitable conclusion of the scene was reached. But her expression made it clear that far from being shocked, she was excited.

CHAPTER 5

Weston awoke to a pounding headache, a stomach which felt as if a dozen dwarfs in hobnail boots were stamping around in it, and a world which moved. The pounding head and painful stomach were not unfamiliar, but the moving world was. Champagne might be the king of drinks, but it provided a knave of a hangover.

He opened his eyes. The ceiling of the bedroom was so low that it was obviously descending; he turned his head and realized that the walls were contracting. He was to be squashed . . . He pulled himself together. Since ceilings didn't descend and walls didn't contract outside the world of Poe, his eyes must be playing him false. Spanish Cava must affect the optic nerves in addition to all the other nerves it hammered. Next time, stick to Scotch . . . He suddenly remembered that it was departure day. Before him lay not a slow recovery at his chosen pace, but an hour and a half bus journey, booking-in queues, plastic food . . . He raised his left hand and after a while the figures of his digital watch ceased to play hopscotch. 10.15. That meant he'd only two hours before departure and he had yet to shave, shower, pack . . . Stephanie's present! It was hell to choose a present for someone who could afford anything she wanted and so he'd put off the purchase until this morning, when inspiration was supposed to strike. Hangover had struck instead. So he'd have to find something in the duty-free shop because she'd never forgive him if he arrived empty-handed. For someone so cold emotionally, she placed extraordinary value on gifts . . .

With two hours—less the time it would take to get ready—he could afford a little longer in bed to relax. Except he couldn't relax because the world continued to move in a way that seemed familiar, yet refused to be identified. There was a regular rhythm and then a quicker up and down and a thud and vibrations whose intensity slowly died away, like ripples in water . . . Water. A boat at sea. He now could place the descending ceiling and contracting walls as deckhead and bulkheads. It was an identification hardly likely to bring mental relief since it was an impossible one. Had the champagne been spiked with LSD—or whatever the latest drug craze was? The distant swishing sound became a bow wave, shredded by wind into spray. The round window became a porthole. The shaft of sunlight moved not because his eyes were false reporters, but because the boat was moving . . .

He sat up, groaned, swivelled round until his legs were over the storm-board. He slid down on to the deck, telling himself that as everything was impossible, beyond this cabin lay orange seas and a green sky. Beyond lay a very short alleyway, a companionway, a saloon luxuriously appointed, a sun-deck at the after end of which was an inflatable slung in davits, and the sea, properly blue.

Well aft of them was a schooner, close-hauled; to port, slightly obscured by the heat haze, lay low land, backed by hills. The boat pitched more heavily than before and he had very hurriedly to reach for a stanchion to keep his balance. He stared at their wake, a creamy line that stretched aft to merge and disappear, and tried to remember boarding. He could not.

After a while he made his way for'd, along the gangway between rails and saloon bulkhead, to come in sight of the wheelhouse. He identified Farley from the back of his head and set of his shoulders. He climbed the ladder and entered the wheelhouse. 'You're not dead, then?' Farley said. 'And there was I about to prepare a canvas shroud and put the last stitch through your nose to make certain you weren't just asleep.'

'What the hell's going on?'

'We're making seventeen knots, the sea's moderate, the wind's east north easterly, force three to four, the swell's slight, and all's well.' Sea was his natural habitat. On land, he was either a slovenly man or an eccentric, depending on the observer's standards; at sea, he was a seaman, Bristol fashion.

'Goddamnit, you know what I mean.' A sea came in at a slightly different angle and the boat rolled as she pitched. Weston had hurriedly to hang on to the second of the two pilot seats. He felt his stomach lurch with the boat.

'By God, you're green about the gills! Fancy a pork chop?' There was a bellow of laughter.

'Why am I here?'

'Because you finally decided to join the human race. When I met you the other day, you seemed a real frag—a wild night out meant dinner at the local golf club. But you sparked last night.'

It added to his inability to make sense of what was happening that Farley should speak in the slang of their schooldays. 'I've got to be at the airport in under two hours.'

'Mission impossible.'

He pointed out to port. 'Where's that?'

'The coast between Puerto Puntos and Cala Besuna.'

'That doesn't mean a damn thing. How long will it take to get back to Restina from the last place you mentioned?'

'By car? I suppose if one put one's foot down, it would take the hour.'

'Then alter course and take me in.'

'No can do.'

'Don't you damn well understand? I'm flying back home today; my wife's expecting me . . .'

'No, she isn't. One can still send telegrams abroad from Spain, so I sent her one explaining that all was well, you'd met an old friend, and you were staying on for a few days. I added lots of love and kisses, but being tactful, didn't mention that you'd also made a new friend. Wives can be very small-minded.'

'One of us is crazy.'

'Good. These days, it's only the crazy who enjoy life. And by the way, I also had a word with the hotel people and they've promised to keep your luggage safe until your return.'

Weston had relaxed his grip on the seat and as the boat pitched and rolled unevenly, he lost his hold and almost fell, managing only at the last moment to save himself. He hauled himself up on to the seat. 'Why?'

'I needed a crew.'

'A crew for what?'

'The trip to Morocco.'

He could just make out the face of the compass. 'We're heading nearly due east. Morocco's to the south.'

'The man's regained a little of his compos! Remember *pons asinorum*? Euclid he say, the safest distance between two points is the longest.'

'What's that mean?'

'The typical guardia civil cabo on coastguard duty is a man of logical, but limited mind. If he sees a boat heading east, he assumes that her destination lies up the coast.'

'If you're trying to hide your destination, you're engaged in something illegal.'

'A very fraggish way of putting things, dear boy.'

'Oh my God!' muttered Weston bitterly. The fact that Farley turned to grin at him with jovial enjoyment added to his rising panic. 'Put me ashore and I'll make my way back to the hotel and I'll forget what you've told me.'

'Scout's honour?'

'Of course.'

'Bullshit.' Farley roared with laughter. As he thrust out his chin, wind came through an open port to pluck at his beard. There was more than a hint of pirate about him.

'I swear—'

'You've never managed anything more serious than a goddamn in your life . . . Laddie, I've been at the wheel for hours and a mug of coffee would be nectar. How about making some? Might bring a touch of life back to your haggard features. The main cock for the gas rings is down at deck level, to for'd.'

'Are you smuggling drugs?'

'That's a bloody fool question.' His tone was suddenly angry, not ironically amused. 'You think I'd dirty my hands with that poison?'

'Whatever you're doing is illegal—'

'Illegal means different things to different people.'

'So what does it mean to you?'

Farley grinned wolfishly.

'I won't have anything to do with it.'

'Scared out of your fragging mind?'

'I don't like breaking the law.'

'Maybe you'll slip your conscience into neutral when you know that before you're two days older, you'll be a sight richer?'

'I wouldn't touch a penny.'

'Not pennies. Twenty thousand dollars.'

'It wouldn't matter if it were a hundred thousand.'

'You remind me of that stupid old sod, Wiles, who tried to teach us English literature. "What we can we will be, Honest Englishmen." . . . Honesty is a commodity like any other. What's your price?' He slid off the seat. 'It seems you're so full of fragging questions I'll have to make the coffee. Take the wheel. Course, zero eight five.'

Farley walked aft and climbed down the companion-way. Weston, moving clumsily, changed seats. They had already swung ten degrees off course. He put on port helm.

As they came back on course, he eased the helm. How the hell was he going to make Farley understand? Anarchic by nature, Farley seemed to hold that conformity, a wish to observe the rules, a desire to keep within the law, were signs of weakness. How to persuade him that they were not? By reasoning? By pleading? He'd shown himself virtu-ally deaf to reason and pleading would surely arouse contempt, not sympathy.

It was a measure of Weston's mental confusion that it took him so long to realize that, initially at least, the answer to the problem lay in his own hands. He put on port helm and brought them round to a due north heading. It was difficult to judge how far away land was, because of the heat haze, but obviously Farley must return long before they closed. So somehow words must be found that would make him understand . . .

He returned, without any coffee, and sat on the starboard seat. He stared for'd, but did not question their altered course. 'You don't want to change your mind about giving a hand?'

'No.'

He leaned across to lay out three photographs on the working surface in front of the wheel. Weston looked down at them and initially saw only a naked man and a naked woman, entwined and making complicated love. Then, with a shock, he identified Jemma and himself.

'I'll admit you surprised me, Aggie. I'd have said you didn't have either the imagination or the technique. I should have remembered what the actress said to the bishop: A dog collar doesn't ensure that dreams of holy places are pure.'

'Who . . . who took them?'

'Marcia. She's a dab hand with a camera.'

'Why?'

'Maybe it turns her on.'

Farley's tone had been mocking. 'They're prostitutes and you paid them?'

'What a bloody Puritan you make yourself out to be except when you're au naturel with Jemma . . . They're not prossies merely happy amateurs who are always ready to buy more time in the Mediterranean sun with the one currency of which they have plenty.'

'You deliberately set me up.'

'Let's say that I placed temptation in your path. And I'll admit that I did so with considerable curiosity. Would righteous virtue prove stronger than sinful vice?'

'And now?'

'That's really up to you.'

'If I don't help you, you'll make use of these?'

'As a man of exemplary common sense, I'm sure you'll see where your interests lie.'

Stephanie found even missionary sex distasteful; these photographs would revolt her.

'From your expression, Aggie, you're thinking about tearing up the photos. By all means do so. Naturally, I have the negatives safely.'

He stared through the port, knowing that he dare not find out if Farley were bluffing.

'Shall we resume course?'

He did not move the wheel.

'Let me reassure your Persil soul. This trip has nothing whatsoever to do with drugs. Indeed, in the strictest sense I rather doubt that there's anything illegal about it.'

He altered course.

*

In the saloon Farley stood and made his way for'd to go up to the wheelhouse to check that the automatic pilot was holding them steady and that no other craft which might be on collision course had come into sight. There was irony, Weston thought, to be found in the fact that at sea Farley was meticulous about keeping a safe watch and so avoiding any risk to others, while on land he was totally careless about such things. Did that make him a first-class seaman or a third-class landlubber?

A couple of minutes later Farley returned and sat. 'The container ship is now hull down and we're well clear of the yacht to port . . . I'm beginning not to like the sky. The cloud looks like there's wind somewhere, but there's nothing in the weather reports. The last thing we want is a gale in this gin palace.'

Weston said nothing.

'Still spitting mad? Relax, laddie. Learn to take life as it arrives. So you've lost a little respectability; you've gained an experience most men only dream about. And before long you'll be able to add in twenty thousand dollars.'

'I've said, I won't—'

'Yeah, yeah. You won't touch one lousy dollar, never mind how strapped for cash you are. I wonder if it'll be quite the same when the money's there in front of you? I reckon principles only flourish in a vacuum.'

'With your lifestyle, that's probably right.'

'Judging by appearances again? A typical inability to realize that the more virtuous the image, the more dedicated the hypocrite . . .' Farley looked at his watch. 'That's five minutes since I was up top, so you can make a check.'

Weston went up to the wheelhouse. The container ship was now little more than a pimple on the horizon and would soon be lost; the yacht was a long way astern; no other vessel had come into sight; the sea had not increased, but the swell was now moderate; the wind was nearer force four than three; course, ninety-one. As he stared out through the port, he tried desperately to work out some way to escape the present situation.

He heard Farley climb up the companionway, then enter the wheelhouse, but did not turn round.

'I wondered if you'd fallen overboard.'

'No such luck.'

'What a mournful bastard you can be!' Farley settled in the starboard seat, belched. 'In a roundabout way, you sometimes remind me of Kate. She has so much faith in essential goodness that she still takes time off to try to reform me.'

'She obviously doesn't know you very well.'

'On the contrary. We lived together for years.'

'Your wife?'

'You can envisage me with one of those? Any woman who'd marry me, I sure as hell wouldn't want to marry . . . No, Kate's my sister.' He brought out from his pocket a pack of cheroots, lit one. 'One of the most loyal women I've met. But pig-headed. After she'd introduced me to Keith and said she was going to marry him, I told her he was a little shit.'

'For which judgement she was no doubt duly grateful.'

He chuckled. 'She can have a tongue like a rapier . . . God knows why she couldn't see the man for what he really was: a born loser. Or maybe it's that which really attracted her—she's always been a sucker for answering a call for help. He hadn't any money, so after the marriage they lived in the cottage in Anstey Cross which had been left to the two of us. She hadn't the money to buy out my half and I thought of giving it to her since I don't spend time in England unless I have to. But then I realized that if she died first he'd take the house and I was damned if I was going to risk that.' He drew on the cheroot, let the smoke trickle out through his nostrils. 'To tell the truth, sometimes I remember the Bramley in full blossom in the middle of the lawn and I'm bloody glad I still own half.'

It was the first time that Weston had ever heard Farley admit to sentimental memories.

'Last year the little shit took off with a mouse of a librarian. D'you know why? He'd at last found someone who was more colourless than he and it gave him a chance to walk tall. All the time he was with Kate, he didn't need a mirror to see how short he stood ... She should have listened to me.'

'Alternatively, you could have kept your opinions to yourself and then she wouldn't have had to marry him to prove her independence. Given time, she might have discovered whether you were right or wrong ... I'm going below to finish my meal.'

'All right, Dr Sigmund.' Farley sounded annoyed. 'And when you're ready, you can go over the stern.'

'Head or feet first?'

That restored his good humour. 'In the inflatable.'

'Why?'

'To paste on a new name and port of registry before we turn south.'

'So that if we're sighted and reported, no one will connect us with *Cristina II* which sailed from Restina?'

'You're learning, laddie, you're learning.'

CHAPTER 6

It was a dark night, with total cloud cover. Both sea and swell had risen and as they lay hove-to, they rolled heavily and there was a constant muttering from the hull—a reassuring sound to any seaman who believed that a silent ship was a dangerous one. The radar screen showed them to be half a mile off the Moroccan coast; a lighthouse, occulting twice every ten seconds, gave a single bearing which, as far as it could, confirmed that position. The chart showed a beach, low land to the east, cliffs to the west, and the small town of Menache beyond a headland.

Farley, who stood in front of the radar screen, said: 'Still nothing?'

'No,' confirmed Weston.

'Goddamnit, if we hang around much longer, someone's bound to become curious. The Moroccans have a couple of fast patrol boats working the coast.' He activated the light in his wristwatch. 'Three-quarters of an hour late. Spaniards can't even make heaven on time. Where the hell are the two of 'em?'

It was the first time that Weston had learned there were two Spaniards to be picked up. Why should Spaniards be smuggled into Spain instead of travelling openly? The obvious answer was that they were either dealing in drugs or were terrorists. Farley had sounded convincing when denying he'd ever have anything to do with drugs, so that left terrorists. He might well feel a kinship with terrorists because they also defied authority. He'd never stop to consider the broken lives, the pain, the deaths, the destruction which might follow in their train . . . And by succumbing to the crude blackmail, he, Weston, could also be said to be closing his eyes to the probable consequences of his actions. Every man had his price, not always measured in money. His was measured in terms of self-respect and, perhaps, self-interest.

Ashore, a red light began to flash—two long, two short, two long. The sequence was repeated. 'There they are.'

'Off you go, then, and bring them back as quick as you like.'

Because they were blacked out, he had to make his way

aft by touch and memory. He was at the stern, untying the painter of the inflatable which was now riding at their stern, when Farley joined him. Farley sniffed the air. 'There's plenty more wind around somewhere. Why the hell haven't the weather experts got hold of it yet?' A landlubber would have derided the notion that coming wind could be detected by sniffing; a seaman knew it could be.

Weston freed the painter, handed the end to Farley. He climbed over the rail and down into the inflatable, a task that called for skill, balance, and luck, if a clumsy over-balance were to be avoided. 'Cast off.' The painter came snaking down, to land across his feet. As he settled the oars in the rowlocks—Farley had vetoed the use of the outboard—the inflatable slowly drifted away from the boat and out to sea in an off-shore current. That would help on the return trip. After rowing for only a couple of minutes, he was certain he was going to be grateful for all the help that was going. The inflatable handled like a square coracle and sweat poured down his face, neck, and back.

The movement of the sea quickened, there was breaking water, and then the bows grounded on sand. As a retreating wave tugged at the inflatable, he scrambled over the side, took hold of the painter, and drew the craft well up on to the gently sloping beach.

He could hear them talking, loudly and with scant regard for security. There seemed little point in his observing a silence and he called out. A man spoke rapidly in Spanish. He walked towards them. 'The boat's along this way.'

He closed sufficiently to make out their forms; there were three of them, not two. 'Who's coming with me?'

More Spanish and then one of them said in English: 'What you want?'

'Which are the two who are sailing with us?'

'All.'

'We're only expecting two of you.'

'All go.'

He silently swore. The inflatable would only take two at a time. 'Then one of you's got to stay behind and I'll come back for him.'

His words were translated by the English speaker and they provoked a bitter argument—at least, that was what it sounded like to him. This finally died away. 'Why you not take all?' came the question. 'Because I can't,' he answered shortly.

There was another argument.

'Hurry up and decide.'

'OK. They go, I wait.'

Two men separated from the third and he led them back to the inflatable. 'Give me a hand to launch her.' They did not move. He swore, manhandled the inflatable back into the water until he was knee deep. 'Come on, then.'

A couple from the Keystone Cops couldn't have acted more clumsily. They stumbled, collided, slipped, splashed, and by the time they were seated at the stern were almost as sodden as if they had been for a swim.

He flashed a torch to advise Farley they were on their way and to switch on a very dim light to guide him, then boarded, with a tenth of the trouble the other two had experienced. One oar was free, the other was not; he pulled hard and as it came free there was a shout of fear from the man who'd been sitting on it, who then moved so precipitately that the inflatable rocked heavily. Weston wondered if it wouldn't be safer to abandon ship.

He fitted the oars in the rowlocks and began to pull. What had been a stiff row on the outward trip became a very hard one on the inward leg despite the advantageous current. His muscles complained bitterly and cramp in his fingers threatened.

Farley's greeting, as they came alongside, was typical. 'Where the hell have you been—on a bloody picnic?' He switched to Spanish. The passengers both stood, the inflatable moved to a swell, and one of them lost his balance and only just saved himself from falling into the sea. Cursing in English, Farley leaned over the rails and, with help from Weston, hauled the two men aboard in turn. 'Hurry it up. Hook on the falls. The crew on the patrol boats can't sleep all night. And if there isn't a gale brewing up, I'm a bloody Dutchman, whatever the weather forecaster doesn't say.'

'Don't you want the other bloke?'

'What are you on about?'

'There were three men waiting. I could only bring two, so I left the third on the beach and said I'd go back for him.'

Farley swung round and spoke to the Spaniards, who stood near the stern, wet and dejected. They replied together and it wasn't until he'd persuaded one of them to be quiet that he was able to understand what was being said. When he did, he swore again. 'Why didn't they bloody well bring along a couple of dozen more whilst they were about it? Go and get the stupid sod.'

Weston cast off and rowed back to the beach. The third Spaniard boarded with a minimum of fuss and none of the clumsiness of his companions. When it became clear that Weston was tiring on the row back, he took one oar and then used that with the forward sweep found in many parts of the Mediterranean to complement Weston's more orthodox stroke. Transferring to *Cristina II*, he was hardly less nimble than Weston.

By the time the inflatable was secured, the motor-cruiser was at full speed. Heading north-east, the sea came in from their port bow and the swell from their beam so that they developed an uneven corkscrewing which repeatedly brought their bows, out of rhythm, down on the crest of a sea with a juddering thud and sheets of spray.

When he entered the saloon Weston saw that two of the passengers were sprawled out in chairs and clearly suffering the symptoms of seasickness. Both were in late middle age and had the puffy features and slack bodies of men who overate and took little exercise. He'd seldom seen less likely terrorists.

The third passenger was in the wheelhouse, standing by the port chair. Considerably younger than his companions, he appeared as physically fit as they did unfit. He spoke rapidly in Spanish. Farley replied briefly, then said to Weston: 'Demanding to know who you are because the crew was supposed to be Spanish. I've told him I only expected two passengers so that makes us all square.'

The Spaniard spoke again and soon he and Farley were arguing heatedly. It was Farley who got the worst of the argument. He said to Weston, his tone angry and careless that the Spaniard would probably understand: 'He's so bloody suspicious, he'd make his father prove he'd fathered a son. I've had to explain that you're a lifelong buddy who was in Restina when Miguel landed himself in hospital, that you're a man I'd trust with my life and wife, and—' He stopped as their bows were caught by a sea and swept to starboard. Hurriedly he put on port helm. 'Go and listen to the local weather report, will you? The radio's tuned to the Alacho station and the shipping forecasts are given on the hour in Spanish and then what they call English.'

The radio was set on a bracket on the for'd bulkhead of the saloon. Weston switched it on. After a couple of minutes of music there was a pause, a series of time pips, and then a Spanish announcer spoke at a speed which telescoped the words. As he waited, he studied the two passengers. Who would be the first to be sick? The announcer switched to English and, contrary to what Farley had implied, was easily understood.

Weston returned to the wheelhouse. 'They've finally decided that there's a storm brewing up. Winds may reach force seven and seas will be moderate to rough.'

'This is no matter?' said the Spaniard.

'A storm always matters,' replied Farley curtly.

'We arrive when is the time?'

'In a boat you arrive when the sea says you can.'

'It is necessary to arrive the time.'

'Then have a word with God.'

'You not understand . . .'

'I understand this much. If the wind and sea get up as the forecast says they're going to, we're heading for the nearest shelter.'

'You do not do that.'

Astonished, Farley looked round at the Spaniard. At that moment a rogue wave slammed into their bows, sending them skidding off course. Cursing, because he prided himself on his helmsmanship, he turned the wheel. They pitched heavily. Weston managed to grab the edge of a working surface for support, but the Spaniard was thrown against the bulkhead.

Farley, shoulders hunched, stared intently through the port as if trying to pierce the darkness to see over the horizon and judge the intensity of the weather.

CHAPTER 7

By dawn the sea was rough and the swell, still running at an angle, moderate to heavy. *Cristina II* was more seaworthy than Farley's earlier and contemptuous description had suggested, but she was not happy and had already lost all the benefit gained from a reduction in speed. She pitched, rolled, and corkscrewed; everything loose had been thrown to the deck; the foredeck frequently took green water; the radar had packed up; and the noises her hull and deck now made were more stressful than comforting.

'Go outside and see what the wind's doing.' Farley had to shout to overcome the noise of the gale.

Weston, choosing a moment when they were on a relatively even keel, went out on the lee side and then edged his way for'd. Legs braced, gripping a handrail, he faced the wind. Within seconds, he was soaked by spray.

He returned into the wheelhouse. 'I'd say it's strengthening.'

The bows rose, slammed down on an oncoming sea. Green water closed over the bows and exploded into a maelstrom of spray which, blown almost horizontal, struck the for'd bulkhead with the noise of distant artillery and temporarily rendered the ports opaque.

'It's time to run for cover,' said Farley. He leaned forward and brought the two throttle controls back to reduce their speed still further. 'Check the chart and give me the course to the nearest harbour.'

The small chart table was against the after bulkhead. Weston switched on the overhead light and studied the opened chart, held in place by raised fiddles. Their last position, plotted from information obtained from the electronic navigator, was timed half an hour previously. He used a pair of dividers to mark off half an hour's estimated run on their present course. The coast to the north and west was inhospitable, with cliffs and open to the weather; to the east, there was a bay and in the centre of this was the small port of San Balieu. He used parallel rulers to plot the course to there, applied the variation.

Moving with short, shuffling steps—the only ones which were safe—he went for'd. 'We've only one option—San Balieu. That means turning and steering zero five one before allowing for deviation.'

Farley shrugged his shoulders; they could not steer a sufficiently accurate course for the deviation of the magnetic compass to be of any practical consequence. 'Stand by.'

Judging the oncoming waves and allowing for their inbuilt unpredictability, using the skill and instinct which came from years of experience, Farley waited for the right moment, then turned the wheel to starboard. For a while it seemed they were going to manage without trouble, then a short, sharp sea, running closer than its predecessors, caught them and sent them into a violent corkscrew which stressed hull and superstructure. With even greater care, he coaxed them through that violence and round on to their new course. 'What's the ETA?' he shouted.

'Three hours, give or take.'

'Then I could do with a break and a coffee. Take the helm.'

Weston stood by the side of the port seat. Farley waited until they were on course with the helm amidships, then slid down on to the deck. Weston sat and took the helm.

The youngest of the three Spaniards came into the wheelhouse, almost losing his footing as the boat rolled. As he grabbed hold of the second seat for support, he spoke excitedly in Spanish. Farley answered and soon they were arguing, the Spaniard gesticulating violently with one hand while he kept a tight hold with the other.

Farley said in English, speaking slowly so that it was clear he wanted the Spaniard to understand: 'The stupid bastard wants to know why we've altered course? Says it doesn't matter what the sea's like, we're to continue as we were. He even wants me to increase speed.'

The Spaniard shouted in English: 'Do as I tell.'

Farley's tone was contemptuous. 'I'm the skipper and at sea a skipper's judge, jury, and executioner. So we don't alter course and we don't increase speed. That leaves us with a chance of making port, always allowing we don't let the boat be caught beam on.'

'I tell you, you change.'

Farley's reply was brief and to the point.

The Spaniard looked as if about to pursue the argument, but in the end said nothing. He stared at Farley for several seconds, his expression angry, suddenly reached under his linen coat to bring out a snub-nosed automatic. 'You change. Now.'

At first Farley was so astonished that he did nothing. Then he hunched his shoulders and, judging the movements of the boat, took a pace forward. 'Give me that and clear out of the wheelhouse or I'll knock you into the bloody scuppers.'

'I shoot.'

'You haven't enough whistle.' Farley's angry scorn prevented any sense of fear.

The Spaniard moved quickly and for once was not caught out by the boat. He put the muzzle of the gun against Weston's neck. 'You change or I shoot.'

The muzzle of the gun seemed to Weston to be made of burning ice. It was the first time that death had come so close to him.

Farley might suffer no fear for himself, but he did for Weston. 'Look, I'm as keen as you are to make our destination on time. But even though this boat is fine in cruising weather, we're in a storm that's building and we must make for shelter. If we resume our previous course and speed, we risk foundering.'

The Spaniard didn't immediately respond. Farley made a mistake. Instead of remaining silent and allowing the violent movements of the boat to underline the truth of his words, he tried to defuse the highly charged situation by making a weak joke. 'Suppose you do arrive a day late? It's an old Spanish custom.'

The Spaniard shouted: 'Change now or I shoot.'

Farley said: 'It looks like he really means it, Aggie, so you'd better do as he says. Come round as quickly as you like.'

In such a sea, it was inadvisable to change course; if one were forced to, then one needed to do so very slowly and very carefully. So Weston could be certain that Farley was telling him to alter course recklessly in the hopes that the resulting violent motions would knock the Spaniard off his feet. He put the wheel hard-a-port.

A sea swept in and for a few seconds their bows actually veered round to starboard; then she responded to the helm and came round. Green water swept over the foredeck and exploded against the wheelhouse bulkhead. They rolled, gunwale under, rolled violently back . . .

Both the Spaniard and Farley, despite his being prepared for what was to happen, were thrown to the deck. Farley was the first to recover and he began to come to his feet; as he did so, his right foot slid on a pencil on the deck and he was brought down again. By the time he'd recovered, the Spaniard was on his feet, the muzzle of the gun once more against Weston's neck. Farley braced himself for the consequences of failure, but it became clear that the Spaniard did not realize that in a storm no helmsman would alter course like that unless he were trying to create mayhem.

The Spaniard looked at his watch. 'How long in time is Restina?' He jabbed Weston's neck.

'I can't say without looking at the chart,' Weston replied thickly.

The Spaniard spoke rapidly in Spanish. Farley carefully crossed to the chart table. The raised fiddles prevented the chart falling, but in addition there was a canvas, sand-filled weight. He moved this down the table before he picked up the dividers, set them at five minutes of latitude, pricked off the distance from their estimated position to Restina. 'Twelve hours.'

'We no arrive until the evening?'

'If we stay on this course at this speed we'll likely not arrive this evening or any other.'

'Quicker.'

'Like hell. We're taking a ridiculous gamble as it is. Go any faster and you may not even have time to say your prayers.'

'More speed or I shoot.'

'Are you bloody blind? Look at the height of the waves.' He pointed with his left arm.

Instinctively the Spaniard stared through a port. Farley picked up the canvas weight and threw it, but as he did so the boat began to roll and he was not quite quick enough to counter the movement. The weight missed the Spaniard's head to slam into the bulkhead. He fired. The bullet struck Farley in the right shoulder and its force flung him backwards so that he fell against the chart table and from there to the deck.

The Spaniard once more jammed the muzzle of the gun against Weston's neck and now the heat was real. 'You make more speed.'

Shocked, Weston leaned forward and edged the two throttle controls very slightly forward.

'More. More.'

He repeated the manœuvre.

'What speed we do now?'

He answered, 'Ten knots,' hoping the Spaniard's nautical sense was so low that he wouldn't realize their increase in revs could not have doubled their speed.

The wind was now gusting up to force eight; the sea was rougher and more confused, often without any sense of rhythm so that it kept breaking on the foredeck, to send water battering aft. On the port side, the for'd section of rails had been bent inboard as if by some casual wrench of a giant's hands; one of the wheelhouse ports had cracked and was letting a small trickle of water through; something in the accommodation was rolling around and this irregularly sent a dull thud through the boat.

Farley lay on the deck, his feet wedged against a locker, his face—where not hidden by his beard—white and strained, his left hand pressing a bloodstained handkerchief against his right shoulder. The Spaniard sat on the starboard seat, gun held in his lap, seemingly completely oblivious of the dangers. On the port seat, Weston summoned up every ounce of skill he'd ever possessed, and some perhaps he hadn't before, to try to nurse them through the gale; anticipating, judging, correcting, using the helm like a driver at the wheel of a formula one Ferrari.

But the violence of the sea increased and it became even more obvious that if they did not alter course and reduce speed, skill and luck would be insufficient to keep them afloat.

'We must head for port,' he said urgently, breaking a long silence.

'No,' replied the Spaniard.

'Then at least let me reduce speed.'

'You change nothing.'

From the deck, Farley shouted: 'Can't you bloody understand that if we go on like this we must founder? What the hell can it matter if we're a day late if the alternative is drowning?'

'We be in Bajols tomorrow.'

'You'll be in hell!' Farley sank back, gripping his shoulder more tightly. Despite himself, he groaned.

The Spaniard was never going to see reason, Weston thought; whatever was motivating him was stronger than any sense of self-preservation. To continue as they were must surely be disastrous, so did he try to wrest the gun away? To make the attempt he'd have to leave the helm— only seconds would be needed for the bows to be thrown off course and, lacking correction, to pay right off so that the boat lay beam on; not much longer for her to be smashed into flotsam. There was only one thing he could do. Alter course to close the coast, but so finely that the alteration went unnoticed. That would at least give them all a better chance of reaching the shore if the boat sank. The kind of chance a passenger had when the engines of a jet airliner flared out at thirty thousand feet.

At 3.15 in the afternoon, after five hours at the helm, tiredness, tension, and fear, finally trapped Weston into a mistake and he failed correctly to read an oncoming wave whose crest was beginning to break. The bows were slammed to starboard with a force that made the hull shudder; a second wave, following immediately behind the first, knocked them gunwale under. As he frantically struggled to put on port helm, a third wave broke over them.

Farley slid across to slam into a bulkhead. The Spaniard was thrown to the deck; the automatic skidded from his hands. Holding himself on the seat with one hand, despite the angle, Weston reached out with the other and moved the throttle controls to try to use the screws to supplement the turning force of the rudder. The bows were invisible in the turmoil of water, but he felt them begin to come round as the boat started to right. Then, when it seemed they might escape, another wave crashed down on them and stove in part of the hull so that the sea began to pour in.

CHAPTER 8

Vessels are like people, they can die quickly or they can die slowly. *Cristina II* died very quickly. More seas swept over her, flooding her hull. The fo'c's'le remained intact to give a degree of buoyancy, but this became a liability, not an asset, as it set up unequal strains that were impossible to contain; after a couple of heavy shudders, the hull split just for'd of the dead weight of the engines. The after part sank immediately; the for'd part floated for a while, but then the bulkhead gave way and it too sank.

One can prepare for a catastrophe, but when it happens it can prove so mind-blowing that all such preparations are forgotten and one's reactions are automatic and made without any conscious logic. At first Weston knew only chaos in which he was a totally passive victim. Then fear overcame the chaos and restored to him the ability to think. He was under water and his lungs were bursting; desperately he kicked out to bring himself to the surface. But the surface was so much part of the chaos that it thrust him back under, he breathed in water, pain speared his lungs and he knew he was going to die and that those who claimed that drowning was a relatively peaceful way to die knew nothing.

His right hand struck something and instinctively he grabbed it. Its buoyancy was sufficient almost to keep him afloat so that now when a wave broke over him, it did not need so much time or energy to force himself back to the surface; and once there, he could raise himself sufficiently to gulp down air that was not half water.

The waves became steeper and fiercer and then he was slammed down on to something and the breath was driven out of his lungs and he gasped and drew in water and choked. He was rolled over and automatically he dug in his fingers to hold himself still and only then realized that beneath him was sand.

As he staggered to his feet, it occurred to him that he'd obviously steered very much closer to the coast than he'd intended; so close, that in another half-hour they might have run aground and that on a coast that was rocky, not sandy.

The house where he found help was owned by an Italian couple. They gave him dry clothes, a couple of brandies, called a doctor, and informed the police. The doctor, with a Spanish indifference to any suffering that was probably not terminal, pronounced him fit and uninjured. The two guardia civil, a cabo and a sargento, with the Spanish police's indifference to almost everything, especially in the early hours of the morning, obviously didn't know what to do with him, but eventually, and after a yawning interpreter had been called, decided to take a statement.

In the sitting-room, to the background noise of wind on the shutters, he futilely wished for more time in which to work out what to say. The problem was all too obvious; the solution, not. Tell the truth about the trip to Morocco and explain why they'd not run for cover when any sane man would have done and it was impossible to judge what the consequences might be. Assume his original guess was correct and the three men were terrorists—despite the appearance of two of them—then he had been guilty of aiding and abetting terrorism. The penalties for that in Spain were probably even tougher than they were in Britain. If the three were, however, merely escaping criminals, he was guilty of aiding and abetting their escape. Instinct told him that few places could be less salubrious than a Moroccan prison. Plead coercion in extenuation and he would either be disbelieved or informed that coercion was no excuse for committing a crime . . .

'Well, señor,' said the sargento impatiently, through the interpreter. He had sad brown eyes, a bushy moustache, and a habit of plucking his right ear.

Weston made up his mind. 'We set sail from Restina . . .' He and Farley had decided to go for a cruise up the coast. They had heard the weather forecast which first mentioned gale force winds, but had not realized how quickly a summer storm could blow up in the Mediterranean and how locally fierce it could become. They ignored the warnings and had suddenly found themselves in the middle of a nasty gale. Then they'd made the fatal mistake of continuing at reduced speed towards Restina instead of making for the nearest port because they'd been invited to a party . . .

The sargento looked at the cabo and shrugged his shoulders, then at Weston with a contempt that was softened by the knowledge that the world was populated by fools. 'Have you any idea what happened to the other señor?'

'None, I'm afraid. We sank so quickly and the sea was so rough . . .'

'Where does Señor Farley live?'

'In or near Restina, but I'm not certain exactly which.'

'You don't know where?'

Weston hastened to disperse any suspicion his answer might have aroused. 'I'm on holiday and only met him by chance and since then we've met each time at my hotel or a café. He never invited me to his place.'

'Does he work?'

'I don't think so.'

The sargento's expression suggested he had definite thoughts on rich, idle foreigners. 'Please describe him.'

The normally difficult task of describing another person was made much easier by Farley's ginger beard; there could not be all that number of men with wild, woolly ginger beards.

'Where do you live in England?'

He gave his address.

'When you return to your hotel, you will please report to the local guardia post and show them your passport.' He stood. 'You are a fortunate man, señor. Had you not been so close to the shore . . .' He shrugged his shoulders.

'Someone will let me know if . . . if my friend's found?'

'Of course. You will be required to identify him.' The sargento, with punctilious courtesy, shook hands; the cabo and the interpreter did the same. The three men left.

'I think you need another drink before I drive you down

to Restina,' said the Italian in a mixture of English and Italian.

He needed it very much.

On Friday morning, he once again walked along the front to the guardia civil post, built as was traditional about a parade square. The inquiry office was to the left of the entrance archway and he went in. The cabo seated behind the desk looked up and shook his head. Farley's body had not been found. Weston explained that he was returning to England the next day and the cabo nodded, but he was fairly certain that the man had not really understood what he'd been saying. He left.

As he walked out from the shadow of the building into the burning sunshine, he wondered whether any of the other four bodies would ever be washed ashore; if Farley's, would the bullet wound be noticed; if one of the three Spaniards, would there be anything to connect his corpse with *Cristina II*? Time, he thought grimly, would be on his side.

CHAPTER 9

By choice, Weston would have lived in the country, but Stephanie had refused even to consider the possibility; for her, culture ceased at the first green field. The taxi drew up outside Francavilla. He sometimes wondered if any other place in England was quite so unsuitably named. Francavilla should have been Mediterranean, all graceful curves, overlooking the sea, not a heavy, cumbersome, late Edwardian house, primarily designed to underline the wealth of the owner. It was one of the few houses left which overlooked the common; most had been knocked down and replaced by luxury flats.

He paid the driver, crossed the pavement, and opened the wrought-iron gate. His car was parked by the side of the garage, whose doors were open to show it was empty. Try as he might, he could never persuade Stephanie to shut the garage when she went out. He walked up the flagstone path, past well-maintained lawn and flowerbeds, to the imposing—or fatuous, depending on one's viewpoint—porch which had Corinthian columns and a pediment. He unlocked the panelled wooden door and stepped into the high-ceilinged hall. The house always seemed to him to smell of ageing dust, but this had to be imagination; Stephanie was almost phobic about dust. He looked at the grandmother clock to the right of the staircase, its carved bannisters the only truly elegant feature in the house; the time was just after six. She was probably at her mother's in Crosford; she sometimes seemed to spend more time there than in her own home. He crossed the hall to the drawing-room—large enough to entertain a couple of rugger teams without a scrum—and went through that to the sitting-room, far more informal in size and style. Between the two windows was a cocktail cabinet, beautifully inlaid, and he poured himself a gin and tonic. He sat on one of the leather chairs. He disliked leather as a furnishing, but she believed that to use it showed taste and an appreciation of quality.

The phone rang. A quick look showed him that the cordless phone wasn't in sight, so he returned to the hall. Judy asked if Stephanie was in, then started to flirt with him. His responses were less than she obviously wished. But he believed that a married man should observe the marriage vows; and that she was a tease, seeking his advances in order to reject them. And if that made him both hypocrite and coward ... He believed a husband should never betray his wife. Jemma and he had left the Kama Sutra standing. He believed a man should honour honesty. Whatever he'd been engaged in in Spain, it had not been honest . . . The call came to an end after he'd refused an invitation to visit Judy the next day when she'd be lonely because Tim was playing golf . . . He went back to the sitting-room, drank, and thought that life was simple, but living was complicated. He could blame Farley for what had happened. But Farley wouldn't have been able to blackmail him into crewing the *Cristina* if he'd lived up to his own standards. Would he have done so had Stephanie not always found sex so distasteful? A man's engagement is a time of delusion; his marriage a time of confusion; his divorce a time of collusion. Certainly, initially he'd deluded himself into thinking that her physical responses would change; and there'd been bitter confusion after marriage when he'd sought to teach her how to find pleasure in what she refused to accept could ever be other than distasteful; but there'd been no collusion over a divorce because she'd flatly refused to consider the possibility. Divorce was a public admission of failure.

Because the doors into the drawing-room and from there into the hall were open, he heard her arrive. He reached the hall as she unlocked the front door and entered. 'Hullo, darling, I'm back.'

'Obviously,' she answered, showing no surprise—for some reason she believed that surprise was one more emotion that a well-bred person did not evince—at finding him at home. She was tall, slim yet shapely, and knew how to move gracefully. Her light brown hair held a natural wave and framed a face that could have been described as classical English—regular, cool, attractive features suggesting calm self-possession. She had a natural dress sense and always looked smart.

'I'm sorry about that sudden change of plans, but I—'

'You forgot that we were having dinner with the Lordons on Tuesday night?'

'I'm afraid I did, yes.'

'I made your apologies. I said you were tied up with work.'

So she had not yet admitted to anyone that he had been made redundant. 'I'm sorry.'

'A sorry forgone is worth two sorries forgiven.'

He found that one of her more irritating sayings. 'Was it a pleasant evening?'

'The Sherstons were there.'

Then for her it had been a pleasant evening. She and Letitia—could anyone have less deserved to be called gladness?—would have swapped misfortunes all night. 'And how have you been?'

'All right, of course.' She had the comforting belief that she could not be troubled by the ills to which lesser mortals were heir.

He made another attempt to lessen the cold resentment. 'I stayed on in Restina because I met Jason, an old schoolfriend. He thought he might be able to help me find a job—he knows people high up in the PR world.'

'And has he succeeded?'

'Not yet. The phone calls he made were pretty unproductive. It seems there are rather a lot of unemployed PRs around at the moment.'

'Rather a waste of time, then.'

'Not necessarily. It might lead to something eventually. Personal contacts are usually worth more than a golden CV . . . I've poured myself a drink. Would you like one?'

'Not now.'

'Have you seen your mother recently?'

'I've been with her today.'

'How is she?'

'Not very well, but she won't admit it.'

Then that was the first time. 'Nothing serious, I hope?'

'I've said she should tell the doctor to give her a complete check-up . . . I'm going to change. I'm rather tired, so we'll go out for a meal.'

'There's no need. I'm not hungry, so bread, cheese, and a salad would be fine.'

She continued up the stairs as if she had not heard him. She was a good cook, and had told him when they were engaged that she enjoyed cooking, but nowadays she seldom missed an opportunity to eat out. He had the feeling that when she cooked for him, she often felt that by doing so she was denying her independence.

She reached the landing and turned into the right-hand corridor. As she disappeared from sight, he wondered how long it would take before he was allowed to forget the Lordons' dinner-party? Back in the sitting-room, he poured himself a second, and stronger, gin and tonic.

At Stephanie's insistence, they had separate beds. On one side of the ornately decorated bedroom was an en-suite bathroom and this they never occupied together; she disliked his seeing her naked. On the other side was a dressing-room which she used, not he.

He climbed into his bed and picked up the paperback on the table, but although he opened it at the marker, he did not immediately begin to read. Should he, he pondered, tell her at least part of what had happened down in Spain, in case there were further consequences? Farley's body might be recovered, when he would probably be called upon to make the identification. The bodies of the other three might be washed ashore and a smart policeman, pondering where they could have come from, might remember *Cristina II* and wonder if the story of being caught unawares in the storm and not making for the nearest harbour showed a stupidity so great . . .

She turned in her bed to face him. 'Garth.' Typically,

she never used the diminutive by which everyone else knew him. 'What is the matter?'

'Nothing,' he answered casually.

'Did something happen in Spain which you haven't told me about?'

Faced with making the decision that only a moment ago had been perplexing him, he chose the easy way out. 'The only unusual event was meeting Jason after umpteen years. He's grown a beard like a bramble patch; I'd never have recognized him, but he knew me right away. He was expelled from St Brede's.'

'Really.'

That was the expression she used, pitched in descending tone, when she didn't want a subject to be pursued. People who were expelled from school were failures. She picked up a book and began to read.

Fifteen minutes later, immediately after she'd switched off her light, he did the same and settled, but for once he did not quickly fall asleep. Could Jason, or one or more of the Spaniards, have survived? Since he had, there must be that possibility. But was it a feasible one? Jason had had a shattered right shoulder and the two oldest Spaniards had looked incapable of anything long before the boat sank, which left only the youngest Spaniard . . . But logic didn't always hold good. Jason, who had always had an air of indestructibility about him, might somehow have managed to struggle ashore. If he had, the police hadn't known about this on Friday . . . He wouldn't be in any hurry to disclose his escape if he couldn't be certain that none of the Spaniards had survived to alert the authorities to whatever had been going on . . .

The more he thought about things, the more certain he became that Farley, had he survived, would for a time lie low. Then how to discover if indeed he were alive? He'd no idea where Farley had lived in, or near, Restina and in the circumstances surely he wouldn't return there anyway? He'd said he was rarely in England, so he wouldn't have a permanent address there ... Weston corrected his thoughts. Farley had talked about his sister, Kate, and the house in which she lived that belonged to the two of them. If he'd survived and was lying low, he'd probably be there—or at least he'd have been in touch with her. But all he'd said about the cottage had been that there was an apple tree in the lawn ... Kate who? Farley had never mentioned her married name. So unless she'd reverted to her maiden name after her husband had taken off with the librarian, there was no way of knowing her present surname ...

His thoughts began to wander. Then, when he was havering on the brink of sleep, the name Anstey Cross came into his mind to jerk him fully awake.

Stephanie was out shopping and it seemed a good moment to try to find out in which part of the country Anstey Cross lay. He phoned the local library which had an information service and was told that there were four towns or villages of that name; two in Kent, one in West Sussex, and the last in Gloucestershire.

He phoned Directory Inquiries and asked if they could trace Katherine or Catherine Farley, who lived in Anstey Cross?—he was sorry, but did not know whether this was West Sussex, Gloucestershire, or Kent. He was told that no one by that name was listed at such an address.

He replaced the receiver. If he wanted to find out if there was any chance Jason had survived, he was going to have to drive to the villages in turn and ask if the Farleys were known.

CHAPTER 10

On Wednesday morning the telephone in the hall rang while Stephanie and Weston were eating breakfast. She looked round the breakfast-room. 'Where's the phone?'

'I'm sorry, I forgot to bring it in. Shall I go and get it?'

'Don't bother. The call's probably for me and I'll take it in the hall.' She spoke with tired resignation, as she usually did when he was at fault.

He watched her leave, buttered a piece of toast and ate. He'd almost finished when the door opened and Mrs Amis looked in. 'We won't be long,' he said.

She turned, without saying anything, and disappeared, forgetting to close the door. He was, he thought, surrounded by difficult women. Mrs Amis came five days a week and did the routine housework, but always as she decided it should be done, not as Stephanie demanded. But Stephanie would never get rid of her because in Baston Common it was one-upmanship to have a daily regularly—even if she were bloody-minded.

Stephanie returned as he poured himself a second cup of coffee and added two spoonfuls of sugar. 'That was Mother,' she said, as she sat. 'She's had a terrible night and is feeling rotten.'

'Has she called the doctor?'

'He left just before she rang. He says there's nothing at all wrong with her. The man's a fool.'

'I don't think he is. I was talking to Bertie, who has him as his doctor, and Bertie says he's a first-class man; but very direct and almost no bedside manner. Personally, I'd prefer a doctor like that rather than—'

'What are you really saying?'

'Nothing except I'm sure he examined your mother very thoroughly.'

'You don't think that she knows whether or not she's ill?'

'It's just possible that she doesn't always.'

'What a filthy thing to say.'

'Old ladies with lots of time and not much to do with it can think themselves ill when they're not.'

'So now you're accusing her of lying?'

'I'm doing nothing more than just trying to point out that it's possible there's no reason for you to get so terribly upset.'

'By your standards, a daughter shouldn't worry about her mother?'

'Not if or when illness is used in an attempt to gain sympathy and attention.'

'God, how you hate her!'

He sighed. 'Of course I don't. Why won't you under-stand—'

'She told me the other day that one of the biggest sorrows of her life is that you dislike her even though she's done everything she could to be friends.'

'To my face, yes.'

'What d'you mean now?'

'When I'm not within earshot, she does everything she can to poison the relationship between you and me because she's jealous.'

'I think you have the most twisted mind I've ever met.' She stood. 'I'm going to drive over to see what I can do for her.' She silently challenged him to object. When it was clear that he was not going to, she hurried out of the room.

He finished his coffee. She and her mother would no doubt spend the day telling each other how much suffering was caused by men . . . It occurred to him that if she was going to be away, he had a chance to try to trace Farley's sister and find out from her whether her brother had survived.

The door to the service passage opened and Mrs Amis stepped inside. 'Still not finished, then?' Her looks were as forceful as her manner; it was difficult to believe that she would ever have needed the support of women's lib.

'I won't be a second.'

When she next spoke, her tone was less aggressive than her words; she quite liked him. 'There's enough to do for two.'

She reminded him of the matron at St Brede's.

As a sweetner to ease the pain of redundancy, the company had given him the Ford Sierra. He drove away from the house twenty minutes after Stephanie and went through London on the South Circular and then down to Canterbury. The most easterly of the two Anstey Crosses in Kent lay seven miles beyond that city. It proved to be an overgrown village in which by far the majority of houses had been built in the past thirty years. There was a local store, in which was a sub-post-office run by a late-middle-aged woman who clearly wore a wig and looked dusty enough to have held the job from youth. She was positive that no one by the name of Farley lived in the area and none of the local inhabitants possessed a ginger beard. He accepted this as proof that Farley's cottage was not in this area.

The day was sunny, with only a few puffballs of cloud, and he chose the back roads to drive to Ashford, a journey which reminded him how lovely the countryside could be. Several miles south of Ashford, the second Anstey Cross was far more the traditional village—half a dozen old cottages, a couple of bungalows, and a pub, set around crossroads.

He went into the pub and ordered a gin and tonic. The landlady was reasonably young, reasonably attractive, and

she had developed a come-on-but-not-too-far manner that
was good for custom. He asked her if she knew anyone by
the name of Farley.

She rested her elbows on the counter and leaned forward
sufficiently that, had he been of an inquisitive mind, he
might have discovered the colour of her underwear. 'Farley?
. . . Can't say the name rings any bells.'

'About my height, but heavier built, with a ginger beard
that sprouts in all directions.'

'Hang on a minute and I'll ask Fred.' She went round
the corner to the other bar.

The landlord, thickset, older than she, appeared. 'You're
asking after a bloke called Farley? There's no one round
here by that name that I knows about. But I can remember
that four, maybe five months back, there was a man came
in and he'd a real bramble-bush of a ginger beard and from
the way he was talking, he was staying at Melton Cottage.
Can't say any more than that, I'm afraid.'

'Have you any idea who lives there?'

The landlord thought for a moment, then called out to
two men who were playing darts. 'What's the name of the
party what lives at Melton Cottage?'

The shorter of the players answered. 'Mrs Stevens.'

'Of course it is! Be forgetting me own name soon.' Then
he added, a shade too casually: 'From all accounts, Mr
Stevens hasn't been around lately.'

Jason had said that his sister's husband had gone off with
a librarian. Weston asked the way to Melton Cottage.

A seven-minute drive brought him to a typical Kentish
farmhouse, set back from the road. He parked by the side
of the garage—an old farm shed from the look of it—walked
down to a wooden gate which needed repainting, set in a
thorn hedge, opened this and went through. He paused to
admire a narrow flowerbed filled with stocks, which ran the
length of the house and was edged with small rocks, all

bizarrely shaped as if they had been subjected to fierce erosion, then continued on round to the south side of the house where the long, sloping roof of peg-tiles came down to within seven feet of the ground. In the centre of the lawn was a well-shaped apple tree; he was far from an expert, but identified it as a Bramley. Farley had talked about a Bramley.

The front door was opened by a woman nearly as tall as he. Red hair, a quieter and warmer shade than Farley's, topped an oval face which held plenty of character, thanks in part to a very firm chin; deep blue eyes, a retroussé nose, and a generous, humorous mouth, softened any suggestion of aggressiveness that the chin might have offered.

He said: 'Mrs Stevens? I'm sorry to bother you, but I'm looking for someone whose married name I'm afraid I don't know. I'm Gary Weston—does that mean anything to you?'

She stared warily at him. 'Should it?'

'Jason and I were at St Brede's together and he might have mentioned me. Are you Jason's sister, Kate?'

'Yes.'

'Then thank goodness I've managed to find you at last.'

'Why have you wanted to?'

'Because . . . I'd better explain from the beginning. I've been on a short holiday at Restina, in Spain, and while there I met Jason by chance. Something which happened means I've needed to talk to you.'

She frowned. 'You'd better come in.'

She led the way through the hall, triangular in shape because of the long sloping roof, and into the sitting-room, which had a beamed ceiling and a large inglenook fireplace. It was furnished with a cheerful disregard for any consistency in style. The curtains had a formless pattern in several bright colours, the loose covers of the two armchairs featured trails of interwoven roses on a light background—the settee did not match—and the carpet was dark and light green measles. The two occasional tables were modern, the kneading trough antique; the small show cabinet might have been either. To the right of the fireplace was a case whose shelves contained an unruly mixture of hardcovers and paperbacks; on the top of this was an ornate, gilded carriage clock. An open newspaper lay on the settee, a ball of wool and a six-inch width of knitting on two blue needles, on a chair. The television was on. It was the room of someone who heeded comfort, not style, and who was indifferent to other people's opinions.

She switched off the television set, sat, carefully smoothing down her cotton frock. 'What happened in Spain?' Her direct manner would have been termed rude by many.

He did not immediately answer the question. 'Have you heard from Jason in the past few days?'

'No.'

'You're quite certain of that?'

'What an extraordinary question. Of course I am.'

'Then I'm afraid I may have some bad news.'

She interlaced her fingers, rested her hands in her lap. 'Bad news concerning Jason?'

'Yes.'

She seemed to thrust her square chin forward. 'What is it?'

She was a fighter, he thought. Whatever he had to say, she was determined to meet it head on. 'Last Saturday we set sail on a short cruise in a motor-boat. While we were at sea a strong gale blew up and caught us and eventually we foundered.'

'And Jason?'

'I managed to get ashore, but there was no sign of him.' He spoke bluntly, believing that bad news was best delivered bluntly.

She turned her head to stare out of the window. 'You're saying he drowned?'

'I'm very sorry, but I'm almost certain he did.'

'You weren't certain when you asked me if I'd heard from him.'

'By Friday, there'd still been no sign of . . . of his body. The only chance was that he'd survived, but the authorities didn't know he had.'

She suddenly unlaced her hands, stood, and hurried past him to the door. A moment later he could hear her cross the room above because the floorboards were laid directly on the beams of the sitting-room. As he looked through the window at the beauty of the simple garden, he wondered bitterly why life had to contain so much sadness.

It was a quarter of an hour before she returned downstairs, eyes reddened. As she sat, she said: 'Sorry about that.'

'I wish I—'

'Wishing doesn't alter anything, does it?'

He was disturbed by the harshness with which she'd spoken.

'Where were you sailing to?'

'Nowhere in particular; just cruising.'

'Do you know what kind of boat she was?'

'An Alder and Farson. I think Jason said she was around sixty feet.'

'Then she was very well equipped?'

'Yes, she was.' He wondered why she was asking these questions? To try to keep her mind off the bad news she'd just been given?

'He hates power so I imagine the boat wasn't his?'

'He told me he'd borrowed her.'

'From whom?'

'I've no idea.'

'She obviously foundered very near the coast, since you reached the shore. Whereabouts exactly was that?'

'The nearest place was Campet.'

'What course were you steering just before you sank?'

He looked at her in astonishment; she returned his gaze, her own expression now openly antagonistic. 'It was two six five as far as I can remember.'

She stood and left the room, quickly to return with a chart which had obviously been well used. She put it down on the settee, after moving the newspaper, studied it, then straightened up. 'Why are you lying to me?'

'I promise you—'

'Before you promise the moon and the stars, let me explain something. Jason dislikes power boats so much that he never sets foot on one unless there's a very good reason—and a cruise to nowhere in particular isn't that. He's sailed practically all his life and so he'd never go to sea without checking the weather forecasts before starting and while under way. Even if the forecasts failed to pinpoint a gale early on—and in the summer in the Med these can almost literally come out of the blue—he has an uncanny instinct for wind. So either he'd never have sailed or else he would have run for cover the moment he heard, or became convinced, that a storm was brewing because he's never foolhardy. Yet according to the course you've just given me, even in the middle of a gale he was not steering for shelter. Only something quite extraordinary would ever stop him doing just that. Just as only extraordinary circumstances can account for your believing he might have survived, yet not told the authorities.'

'That's only because I was hoping against hope.'

'I see. And the reason for his not making for safety?'

'I'm sorry you don't seem to believe me, Mrs Stevens, but it happened as I've said.'

'Then you'd better go.' Tears began to well out of her eyes.

He left.

*

He drove round the south side of the common, slowed as he approached Francavilla and then, since the pavement was clear, ran up into the drive to park to the side of the garage. The Mercedes was back, the garage doors were left open. He locked up his car, shut and locked the garage doors, walked round to the porch. As he unlocked the front door, he wondered what sort of a mood he'd find her in? Often after a visit to her mother she was even sharper than usual.

He stepped inside, turned to close the front door, and saw that on the floor by the staircase was a bundle of clothes. It was so unlike Stephanie to leave anything lying around that he continued to study them. And now, among them, he made out a head and two arms . . .

CHAPTER 11

'I can give you some pills that will help you through the next few days,' said the doctor.

Weston shook his head. He watched the men carry the green body-bag, which sagged in the middle, across to the front door and was appalled by the lack of dignity of Stephanie's final departure from the house of which she had been so proud.

'If you change your mind, give me a ring; at the house, if it's outside normal hours.'

'Thanks.'

The doctor left. Bewildered, not thinking about what he was doing, Weston carried out his usual routine. He locked and bolted the front door, checked all window catches, locked and bolted the two back doors. When he returned to the hall, he stared at the stained parquet flooring, beyond the Kashan carpet, and suffered bitter sorrow over the thought that while she had been alive he had not tried harder, as he could have done, to make their marriage a happy success.

Mrs Amis had a key to the back door which gave direct access to the service passage and since that was normally unbolted by the time she arrived, she was able to let herself in. But on Thursday morning, she found that the door remained bolted. It was not without pleasure that she pressed the bell several times.

Weston awoke with a start, his mind initially clouded. He saw that the second bed had the cover drawn over it and was astonished that Stephanie could have bathed, dressed, and made the bed without waking him . . . His mind cleared and he remembered that the bed had not been slept in.

The bell continued to ring. He threw back the bedclothes, climbed out of bed, went across to the right-hand built-in cupboard and brought out the hand-embroidered silk Chinese dressing-gown Stephanie had given him at Christmas two years previously. About to put this on, he suddenly suffered an overwhelming repugnance to do so. He exchanged it for the simple cotton one which dated from before their marriage.

He went downstairs, through the kitchen and pantry, to the passage and unbolted the door. Mrs Amis, wearing a patterned frock that didn't suit her, entered and said, as he shut the door: 'Had a heavy night of it, Mr W?' She would never have spoken in that jocular tone to Stephanie.

'There's been a very serious accident. Mrs Weston fell downstairs yesterday and I'm afraid she died.'

The magnitude of the tragedy shocked her, especially as she had been expecting nothing more serious than the report of some favourite vase broken. 'Oh my God!' She was a rough woman because she had had a rough life, but she had never lost sympathy for anyone who suffered. She tried to express her sorrow and if her words were trite, the emotion behind them was not.

He thanked her, turned to the doorway into the kitchen, checked himself. 'It'll probably be best if you return home today.'

'There must be something I can do to help.'

He hesitated, then said: 'You could clean up the hall.'

'Don't you worry.' She tried not to show her repugnance at the thought of what might face her. 'Don't mind me asking, do you, but have you told Mrs Badger?'

'My God, no.'

'Best do that right away.'

He went into the kitchen, across the narrow passage into the hall, and from there into the drawing-room. The cordless phone was on a piecrust table by the side of the chair on which Stephanie had always sat. He picked it up, punched out the number.

At first the call was not answered and he thought with cowardly relief that she must be out. But as he was about to switch off, she said in her tight, over-articulated voice: 'This is Crosford one seven six one three five.'

'Monica, it's Gary.'

'Good morning, Gary. Isn't it a lovely day?'

Her dislike of him could be measured by her unfailing, inane politeness. 'I've some very bad news.'

'It's . . . Stephanie?'

'I'm afraid she's had a very serious accident.'

'No,' she shrieked, in a despairing attempt to defy fate by denying it.

'She fell from the landing . . .'

'Which hospital is she in? What do the doctors say?'

'That she can't have suffered because she landed on her head; death was instantaneous.'

'You don't mean . . . You can't . . . She can't be dead . . .' Her words became jumbled, at times incoherent.

But then she became more coherent and he understood that she was accusing him of having killed Stephanie.

The doctor was sufficiently old-fashioned still to be concerned about his patients. He called at Francavilla on his way home to lunch. 'I wanted to see if you'd decided you'd like something to help?'

'I'm managing,' replied Weston.

'You know, there are times when the stiff upper lip and suffering-is-good-for-you is just plain damned stupid.'

'But difficult to overcome when one went to St Brede's.'

'Yes, well the English public schools have a lot to answer for, quite apart from Burgess and Maclean . . . Have you thought about making the arrangements?'

The question perplexed Weston.

'The funeral,' explained the doctor. 'In my experience, the sooner that's dealt with and out of the way, the better. Time only makes it more difficult. There'll have to be a PM, of course, since I hadn't seen your wife for medical reasons for many months and this was an accident, but that'll be only a formality. The local firm of undertakers, Rainer and Desmond, are very competent and tactful. If you've no one else in mind, perhaps you'd like me to have a word with them on your behalf?'

'If you would.'

'Did your wife ever express a preference for burial or cremation?'

'She never talked about death.'

'There's nothing in her will?'

'I haven't checked.'

'It would be an idea to do so and then let them know.'

The doctor left. Weston shut the front door, went through to the sitting-room where he poured himself a drink. He was surprised to discover how little he knew about all the problems which followed death.

Detective-Constable Turner parked the CID Escort in the car park, took the lift up to the fourth floor of divisional HQ. A short walk brought him to the CID general room where he sat down at his desk, stared unseeingly at the large baize-covered notice board, and thought about Pauline.

There was a shout from the doorway. 'Phil—I want a word.' He looked across just in time to see the Detective-Sergeant disappear.

Turner sighed. Was Pauline seeing that smooth bastard at the tennis club who drove around in a Morgan, or was she really busy at home, helping her mother, as she claimed? He'd never liked tennis.

He stood, left the room, and went along the corridor to the Detective-Sergeant's room. Waters was seated behind his desk, reading through a report. He was a typical PW case—pension-watching. More concerned in avoiding trouble than in promoting criminal investigations because he'd only just over a year to go before retirement.

Waters used a pencil to correct a spelling, then looked up. 'There's a report in from Crosford; a Mrs Badger is claiming that her son-in-law murdered her daughter.'

'So why don't Crosford ask him?'

A brief expression of irritation crossed Waters's square, heavy face. 'The son-in-law lives in our ground, that's why. His name's Weston and he's at Francavilla, Trefoil Road, Baston Common.'

'Pansy name for a house.'

'You'd rather Seaview? The daughter's name is Stephanie. Yesterday afternoon—at four-sixteen if a smashed watch can be relied upon—she fell from the landing on to her head and died. The husband came home to find her.'

'Where was the mother?'

'In her place, in Crosford.'

'Then how can she know enough to get shouting?'

'That's what you're going to find out.'

'Sarge, if we stopped off to investigate every mother-in-law's complaint, we'd be working twenty-five hours a day and getting nowhere.'

'This one's shouting murder, so we have to listen. Get moving.'

Turner returned to the general room, had a quick word with another DC, went over to his desk and sat. He phoned the coroner's officer. 'Hi, Mac, how's life?'

'The name's Tom and it's lousy.'

'No one gets it right every time. What can you tell me about Mrs Stephanie Weston?'

'Sweet FA.'

'Come on. She died yesterday in an accident, so-called, so she must be around somewhere.'

'Hang on.'

He leaned back in the chair and put his feet up on the desk. If Pauline were trying to play him off against that tennis jerk, he'd make out he was having a closer look at the brunette in the baker's whose eyes signalled that she was willing if he was . . .

'Are you there?'

'I'm not off to Bermuda until tomorrow.'

'Mrs Weston came in yesterday evening. The acceptance note merely says accidental fall resulting in fatal head injuries. No one's carried out the preliminary examination yet. Where's your interest?'

'Her mother's shouting the husband murdered her. Could it have been murder, not accident?'

'Ask the pathologist, not me.'

'Will you tell him to make a really careful PM?'

'And so suggest he doesn't always? Not bloody likely.'

*

The coroner's officer rang on Saturday morning. 'About Mrs Weston.'

Turner, trying to fill in a T24 form correctly, had to shake his mind to identify the case.

'There was time today for the initial, external examination. Injuries to the head appear to be consistent with falling on to a solid surface. There are no other signs of injury except for bruising, sustained immediately before death, on the stomach. This is in the form of a horizontal line at a height of three feet three inches.'

'Any suggestions as to what might have caused that?'

'A blow from something solid, probably rounded; say a thickish pole.'

'What about if she were leaning hard on banisters and overbalanced?'

'It would need more force than that.'

'All right. She was running, went into them and overbalanced.'

'Possible.'

'Can't you be more definite?'

'Not before the full PM is carried out and even then it may be impossible to give a definite answer.'

'You don't make life easy.'

When the call was over, Turner went along to the Detective-Sergeant's room, saw that Detective-Inspector Rentlow was also there and turned away.

'Yes?' the DI called out.

He returned to the doorway. 'It's not important, sir.'

'A typical DC's assessment of vital information.'

Sarcastic bastard, Turner thought.

'Well, what is so unimportant?'

'The coroner's officer has rung, sir. An external examination of Mrs Weston has been carried out, but not the full PM as yet. Head injuries are consistent with the fall. Additionally, there's horizontal bruising across her stomach which was probably caused either by a blow with something like a solid stick or from her running very hard into something like the banisters immediately before her death.'

'Not enough there to say whether it was murder, is there, as the mother insists?'

'No, sir. We have to wait for the full PM.'

'Well, what's your next move?'

'I thought I'd measure the height of the banisters in the house.'

'A man of mental initiative!'

Turner left. It was popularly believed that Rentlow was marked out for quick promotion; since this would take him away from divisional HQ, there were many who looked forward to the day. It wasn't that he worked them any harder than another DI would, or that he refused to stand by them when there was trouble—on the contrary, he regarded the CID as a team and therefore that it was his job to defend them against the outside world—but it seemed impossible to pin down what kind of a man he really was. And unless one could identify a man's weaknesses, one was always at a disadvantage.

One of the hardest things to accept, since indifference mocked emotions, was that however great one's distress, the world kept turning. Weston, slumped in a chair in the sitting-room, stared at the television set, but took in nothing of what he saw and heard. He suffered more guilt than sorrow. Self-honest, he accepted the fact that the marriage had not been a happy one and her death was not the overwhelming loss it could have been; but as in his mind he played through scenes from the past, he identified time after time when he might have brought them closer together had he been prepared to make himself more the kind of man she had wanted him to be . . .

The front doorbell rang. He decided to ignore it. Friends

had called to offer their condolences and it was difficult to decide who had been the more embarrassed, they or he. Because death was the modern taboo, no one knew how to cope with it.

The bell rang again; then for a third time. He stood, went through to the hall and opened the front door, prepared to hear murmured words of mournful sympathy and in return to murmur words of mournful gratitude.

'Mr Weston? My name's Detective-Constable Turner. I'm sorry to have to bother you at such a time, but I need a word with you.'

The apology had been made briskly, but he preferred it that way. He watched Turner enter. Slightly younger than himself, more solidly built, and almost certainly in better physical condition, with a square face that not even a girl-friend would call handsome, but which contained con-siderable character. He closed the door.

'I'm here because I'm afraid that after any fatal accident in the house, we have to determine the circumstances. It's so that the causes can be analysed and later on advice be drawn up which will help avoid their repetition. I'll be as brief as possible.' He turned and looked along the hall at the stairs and the open landing above. 'Did your wife fall from up there?'

'Yes.'

'And you weren't here at the time?'

'No.'

'You were at work, I suppose?'

'No . . . What's it matter where I was?'

'Sorry, Mr Weston, but like I said, I have to ask the questions, whether I want to, or not. Had your wife recently had any fainting fits or complained of dizzy spells?'

'No. But if you want to find out her medical history, wouldn't it be best to speak to her doctor?'

'It's just that sometimes people hang back from seeing

their doctors because they're afraid of learning that something really is wrong . . . I wonder if you'd mind if I went up and measured the height of the banisters?'

'Why?'

'It could be important to establish if perhaps they're a little low. A recommendation for a higher minimum height might save lives in the future.'

Turner waited, then when Weston remained silent he crossed the hall and climbed the stairs. Using a spring-loaded metal tape, he measured the height of the solid top rail of the banisters, oval in shape. From the top of the thick pile carpet to the point of greatest projection was three feet four inches. He straightened up, pressed the button which allowed the tape to rewind, and studied the hall beyond the banisters. There was nothing—no picture which might have needed straightening, no light which might have needed a new bulb—that the dead woman could have been reaching out to.

He returned downstairs. 'Thanks for your help. I'll let myself out.'

Weston briefly and cynically thought that the information gained would almost certainly do nothing but gather dust, and returned to the sitting-room. The television programme had changed and a nature film was showing. He watched it, but at the end could have said very little about it.

CHAPTER 12

'Well?' said Waters.

Turner settled on the edge of the Detective-Sergeant's desk. 'Allow for the extra height of shoes and the depression of the carpet and the measurements fit.'

Waters scratched the top of his head, at the point of maximum baldness. 'Could be interesting.'

'Equally interesting, there's a three hundred Mercedes in the garage and a Sierra outside, so there's money knocking around.'

'You don't need to see a Mercedes to know that. Any of the houses with a big garden overlooking the common is worth the right side of three-quarters of a million.'

Turner whistled. 'As much as that?'

'Knock the house down and build a block of luxury flats in the grounds and you've doubled your money or better.'

'How do I become a property developer? ... Sarge, there's more to come. It looks like he maybe doesn't do any work.'

'So he was at home when you called. Would you rush back to the office after you'd found your wife dead?'

'I'm not going by that. He told me he wasn't at work the day his wife died. What if she had all the money and he's been living off her? That sets up a strong motive for murder.'

'There's no one can accuse you of lacking imagination ... Don't forget Agag.'

'I can't, since I've never heard of him.'

'He trod very delicately.'

'All I'm saying is—'

'All you're saying is, you're happy to jump to conclusions.'

'You don't reckon it's worth finding out who had the money, him or her?'

'We need to find out, sure, but very discreetly so he doesn't become paranoiac.'

'Any suggestions how we manage that?'

'Determine who owns the house. I did hear that the Land Registry has been opened up to everyone. Failing that, try the local council and ask them to look through their old ratings lists. If the house is in her name, not his, you know who was the money-bags.' Waters yawned. 'Now you've met him, what do you make of him?'

'Hard to say. I mean, I was only in the place for a short while.'

'Was he in a state of shock?'

'He certainly wasn't all smiles. But if my wife had just taken a nose-dive into oblivion, I reckon I'd look more shattered than him.'

'You're sure it's not a case of stiff upper lip? You don't want to judge too much by appearances, you know. I remember questioning a bloke who seemed not to have a care in the world and he committed suicide a few hours later.'

'Cause and effect, Sarge; cause and effect.'

The offices of Rainer and Desmond were half way along Prince's Street, a little on from the underground station. Discretion was their hallmark, both in the window display of a single white arum lily in a Waterford vase before a black pleated backdrop, and in the reception area which had comfortable furnishings, indirect lighting, and background music which was serious but not funereal.

The receptionist, middle-aged, motherly, dressed quietly but not drably, showed Weston into the office and introduced him to the manager.

Brisson came round the desk and shook hands. 'Good morning, Mr Weston. Please accept my condolences,' he said, sounding sincere and not as if reciting words which had long since lost any meaning for him. 'Do have a seat.'

Weston settled on the chair in front of the desk. 'Dr Pearson said he'd asked you to make all arrangements and you'd promised to be in touch about the day. I've not heard anything.' He had not meant to sound belligerent, but was aware that he had.

'The reason for that, Mr Weston, is that we have not yet been given a date.'

'I don't understand.'

Brisson spoke carefully. 'When there has to be a post-mortem, I'm afraid there can be no funeral until the authorities give permission for it to go ahead.'

'And they haven't?'

'Not yet.'

'Why not?'

'I'm afraid I can't say. The authorities will never discuss the matter.'

'You haven't specifically asked them?'

'No, because it will—'

'If you haven't, I will.'

'Mr Weston, I can assure you that you will learn nothing and only cause yourself considerable distress. In these circumstances, they are never prepared to give details.'

'What do you mean—"in these circumstances"?'

For the first time Brisson showed signs of uneasiness. 'When there is any doubt . . .' He came to a stop, hesitated, started again. 'Until they are certain there are no further questions to be answered, they will neither release the body, nor explain the delay.'

'How can there be any question concerning my wife's death? Could anything be more straightforward? She fell from the landing. Only a fool—' He stopped abruptly. 'I'm sorry.'

'There is no need to apologize.'

Weston stood. 'You'll let me know as soon as they say the funeral can go ahead?'

'I'll be in touch immediately I hear.'

He left, walked down the road towards his parked car, stopped in front of the Boar's Head. Normally, he was not a pubby man, but for him this was not a normal time. He went into the saloon bar and ordered a gin and tonic from the busty woman behind the bar. As he drank, he wondered why life seemed to delight in putting the boot into someone who was already down. He'd been dreading the funeral, yet ready to welcome it because he accepted that its very finality would bring a sense of some relief. Now he was being denied even that relief because some bloody bureaucrat couldn't be bothered to do his work.

Turner rang the front door bell of Francavilla and then turned and looked out from the porch at the front garden. Was the Detective-Sergeant right when he said the place was worth the right side of three-quarters of a million? He wasn't naïve, but it always astonished him that one man could live in a house valued at hundreds of thousands while for another ninety-nine it would be a hell of a struggle to afford the necessary mortgage for one that cost under a hundred thousand—well under, if he were a lowly copper. Did that bastard tennis-player with a Morgan own a large and luxurious house? Surely Pauline was not the kind of girl to let her emotions be swayed by sordid financial considerations?

'Yes?'

He swung round to face a woman who reminded him of the photograph of his Great-Aunt Matilda who'd worked in Grimsby, gutting fish, and who was reputed to have smoked cigars. 'Is Mr Weston in?'

'No,' said Mrs Amis.

'Then d'you know when he'll be back?'

'Can't say.'

'I guess you work here?'

'What's it to you?'

'The name's Detective-Constable Turner.'

She was unimpressed.

'Maybe I could have a bit of a word with you?'

'What about?'

'This and that. You see, I have to draw up a report on the accident and need to find out a few facts.'

'Can't tell you nothing. Didn't even know about it until Mr W comes and says what's happened. Give me quite a turn.'

She didn't look like a woman to 'have turns'. 'I'm sure it did. Especially as you'll have liked her a lot?'

'Who says?'

'Then you didn't like her? A sharp employer wanting her pound of work?'

Mrs Amis's mouth tightened. 'How's that any of your business?'

'Quite right, it isn't,' he agreed cheerfully. 'But I don't suppose you'll find any objection to saying how fit and well she was?'

'What d'you mean?'

'Did you know her to have a dizzy spell recently?'

'No.'

'Or talk about not feeling well?'

'That's about all she didn't complain of.'

'Never satisfied? I've a detective-inspector that's the same. He'll be moaning if they don't shut the pearly gates after him the way he wants ... What about me stepping inside instead of standing out here?' He smiled.

She hesitated, then finally stood to one side. As soon as he was inside, she closed the door. 'I suppose you'd not say no to a cup of coffee?'

'You're right enough there.'

'Never met a man what would, just so long as it's in working hours.'

He followed her into the kitchen, whistled. 'I've not seen this much equipment outside a shop before.'

'I don't suppose you have. Barmy, I say, since she don't like cooking. But if you don't know what to do with all your money ...' She opened a cupboard and brought out a glass jar of ground coffee. A coffee-maker was by the side of the split level cooker and she filled it from the tap.

'Rolling in the necessary, is he?'

'Not him. Hasn't even got a job since he were made redundant.'

'When was that?'

'Not so long ago—like just before he went on holiday.'

'So she's the one with all the loot?' He needn't, he thought, have initiated inquiries to discover to whom the house belonged.

She filled the machine with coffee, screwed the two halves together, set it on the ceramic hob and switched on the electricity. 'How about a chocolate biscuit?'

'I can never say no to one of them.'

'No more could my Alf.'

One of the ways of pursuing a successful interrogation while hiding the fact that that was what it was, was to appear to show interest in unconnected matters. 'He's your husband?'

'Died eight years back. Poorly one day and was taken to hospital and in four days he was dead.' She spoke without any emotion and it would have been easy to assume that his death had left her virtually unmoved. But she still could not think of him without a lurch in her mind. She crossed to another cupboard, brought out a tin, opened this and put it on the table. 'They're Mr W's favourites. So they should be, seeing what they cost.'

He helped himself to one. He had expected a foie gras of a biscuit, but to his disappointment, since he had a very sweet tooth, found that the chocolate was not only plain, it was slightly bitter. 'I suppose she inherited all her money?'

'She didn't get it on the streets, that's for sure. Though maybe he'd have been happier if she had!' She laughed heartily.

For someone who'd earlier refused to begin to discuss the personality of her employer, she was proving to be remarkably forthcoming, he thought sardonically. 'Like that, was it?'

'Single beds and plenty of room between 'em.'

'Well, they do say you can't have everything.'

The coffee bubbled and she switched off the electricity. She set on the table a chased silver sugar bowl and a bottle of milk, filled two mugs with coffee, passed him one. 'Pull up a chair and have another biscuit.'

They both sat. Despite his previous disappointment, he helped himself to another biscuit. 'So they didn't always get on all that smoothly?'

'Are you married?'

'Not yet.'

'Then you've still got to learn it ain't always love and kisses.'

'They had rows?'

'Of course they did.'

'What about?'

'How would I know. I ain't interested enough in their doings to keep my ear to a keyhole. It's just that sometimes I couldn't but know they was rowing.'

'Why d'you think they did?'

'Because she was the kind of woman she was. Always quick to remind him it was her with the money. Even when he had a job, she'd get at him for not earning enough. Straight, I felt sorry for him. A man needs to be able to prove he's someone and with her that wasn't easy.'

'It sounds as if it must have been nigh impossible.'

'Being made redundant hurt him really hard and not just because she went for him more'n usual. Couldn't see what she was doing to his pride. He said he needed to get right away from everything for a bit, but she wouldn't go with him because it was one of them package holidays. Probably thought she'd catch something nasty if she had to mix with people who'd be on that sort of holiday.'

'They even rowed over that?'

She sipped her coffee, put the mug down and added another spoonful of sugar. 'She wanted to go somewhere decent and she'd pay. Couldn't see that that was rubbishing him even more. It's the only time I've heard him really going for her. For my money, he ought to have done that much more often.'

'You're all for men's lib?'

'Most of 'em don't need any more liberty that they already take.'

He laughed. 'So how were things when he returned from the holiday he took on his own?'

'In the deep freeze, that's where. He'd dared to do something he wanted to do and she didn't.'

'And the relationship hadn't improved by last Wednesday?'

'I can tell you, she was real sharp that morning. Went for him because her mother moaned about being ill and he tried to say her mother only did that to get attention.'

'One way and another, it doesn't sound as if it was a very happy marriage?'

'Must've had his eyes closed when he first met her. Or else he didn't know much about women.'

'What man does?' He helped himself to a third biscuit; an acquired taste he was rapidly acquiring.

Waters, standing in front of the window of his office and looking out, jingled some coins in his right-hand trouser pocket.

'It's beginning to look hot,' said Turner.

He turned round. 'You don't think that maybe you're seeing things too pat?'

'Jeeze, Sarge, it's all there. The marriage was as cold as

Boxing Day turkey, he'd lost his job and was skint, she had big money and didn't hesitate to rub his face in that fact ... I tell you, dig a bit deeper and we'll find a little blonde tucked away who keeps him in working condition and has been wondering how the title, the second Mrs Weston, will fit.'

'Maybe. So you'd better start digging.'

'Give me a break and let someone else labour. How can I handle any more workload when I've twice as much as I can cope with already?'

'Squeeze it in, lad. Like a forty-six woman facing a thirty-six bra.'

CHAPTER 13

Weston put the coffee-maker on the stove and switched on the electricity. He set two cups and saucers on a tray, added butter, black cherry jam, honey, sugar, milk, the bread-board with half a wholemeal loaf on it, and Stephanie's letters. It was only as he stood in the breakfast-room, about to set the table, that he realized there was no longer any need for two places. He was both bewildered and angered by his mistake. He carried the tray back to the kitchen and then laid one place at the table there. In no circumstances would she have ever considered eating breakfast in the kitchen.

As he waited for the coffee to make, he opened the first of her letters, something he had never done before, first because he had always respected another person's privacy, secondly because she had been so secretive a person that she had never even discussed the contents of her letters with him. The envelope contained an invitation to a fashion show in three weeks' time.

The coffee-machine began to hiss. He crossed to the stove, switched off the electricity, poured himself a cup of coffee, sat. He cut a slice of bread, buttered and spread jam on it. As he ate, he opened her second letter. Her stockbrokers had sold a block of shares because the analysts reckoned that the company was now on a plateau and profits were unlikely to rise, might even fall. As usual, the proceeds—nineteen thousand and fifty-four pounds—would be put on deposit until another suitable investment was identified. He drank some coffee and ruminated on the fact that he'd no idea how wealthy she had been. The extent of her investments had been just one more personal detail she'd jealously guarded. Not for the first time, he wondered if the reason for her phobic secrecy had as its base a fear of emotionally exposing herself.

Mrs Amis arrived before he'd finished the meal and when she entered the kitchen and saw him eating there, she stared with amazement. Then, with a smile that suggested sardonic amusement lurking around her mouth, she asked him if he wanted her to clean the drawing-room and dining-room as she normally did on a Tuesday. He replied that it seemed best to stick with the routine. She collected brush, dustpan, duster and vacuum cleaner from the utility room and carried them through.

He cleared the table, picked up the stockbroker's letter and went along to the library. There were two desks, both partners', one of which had been hers. He dropped the letter on the top, checked the drawers on either side and found them locked. He went upstairs to their bedroom. Her handbag lay on the elaborate dressing-table. Again conscious of how unusual his action was, he opened the handbag and searched through the contents. The keys to the desk were in one of the zip compartments.

He was not surprised to find that all her papers were very carefully filed—she had been obsessively tidy. He opened the file marked 'investment valuations'. The figures of the latest valuation astounded him. Her portfolio had a total market value of just over one and a half million pounds.

He heard the front doorbell. Then, because all the doors through to the hall were open, he heard the murmur of voices, without being able to distinguish the words.

There was a shout. 'Mr W. It's for you.'

He put the valuation back in the folder and the folder in the drawer. He crossed to the further door and stepped into the hall. Turner stood near the front door. There was, he thought, a suggestion of aggressiveness about the Detective-Constable even when he was standing silent. ''Morning.'

'Good morning, Mr Weston. I had to pass, so I thought I'd save a journey and drop in. Hope it's not too early for you?'

'Far from it. And I'm glad you've come because there's something I want to know.'

'Ready to help if I can.'

Mrs Amis was standing by the doorway into the service corridor. 'We'll go through to the sitting-room.' He led the way, stood in front of the fireplace and waited while Turner settled in one of the armchairs. 'I want to know why the post-mortem hasn't been completed so that the funeral can take place.'

'I really can't answer that. It's nothing to do with us.'

'I can't damn well see the need for one in the first place.'

'It's the law.'

'All right, I can't damn well see why the law says there has to be one. What can be more straightforward than the accident?'

'Well, as a matter of fact it has raised a question or two.'

'How d'you mean?'

'Like why did she fall?'

'She had a dizzy spell, she tripped and over-balanced . . . How does any accident happen?'

'You yourself told me she'd no history of dizziness.'

'Does that stop her suffering it a first time?'

'Of course not.'

'Is that the only question?'

'There is another. Although a full PM hasn't yet been conducted, a preliminary examination has been. There was bruising on your wife's stomach. To your knowledge, had she recently suffered any sort of a blow which could have been responsible for that?'

'No, she hadn't. Was that why you insisted on measuring the height of the banisters?'

'That's right.'

'What did you discover?'

'The two heights appear to match.'

'Which suggests what?'

'One explanation would be that she ran into the banisters at a very considerable speed and this caused her to over-balance and fall.'

'Why should she run across the landing?'

'The question I was about to ask you.'

'My answer is that it's a ridiculous question.'

'Not necessarily. Maybe she was trying to escape from something or someone.'

Because the implication of the question was so abhor-rently unexpected, it took Weston a couple of seconds to realize what this was. Then he said, his voice high: 'Are you suggesting she was attacked?'

'I'm afraid it's a possibility we have to consider,'

'Impossible!' Weston crossed from the fireplace to slump down on the nearest armchair. 'I tell you, impossible.'

'There weren't any signs of a forced entry, I know, but a really smart villain can make them very hard to find. I think you were asked to check if anything in the house was missing—have you done that?'

'Nothing is.'

'Then I imagine we can forget a smart villain since he'd not have left empty-handed. And, of course, an unsmart tearaway would have left obvious traces . . . Tell me, had your wife by any chance recently had a row with anyone?'

'D'you think that if she had, that person would have broken in here and hounded her to her death?'

'It can happen.' He stood. 'I won't bother you any longer. Thanks for your cooperation.' He crossed towards the doorway, came to a stop, turned. 'There is one more thing. Purely for the records, where were you on Wednesday afternoon, let's say between three and five?'

'Why d'you ask?'

'My sarge is the kind of bloke who gives a twenty p. piece for something costing nineteen and checks the change three times.'

Turner had spoken so casually that Weston accepted that the information really was unimportant. 'I was down in Anstey Cross.'

'Can't say I know where that is.'

'In Kent; south of Ashford.'

'They say Kent used to be a lovely county before the motorways, Channel tunnel, and super railway . . . Just to make my sarge really happy, can I have a name?'

'I've just told you; Anstey Cross.'

'The name of whoever you were with.'

'Mrs Stevens.'

'Thanks. Then that does sack everything up nice and tight. Good to have had a chat.'

CHAPTER 14

Detective-Constable Ford parked the CID Metro in front of the garage at Melton Cottage and climbed out. There was a familiar feeling of discomfort in his stomach and an acidic sensation at the back of his throat and he brought a plastic bottle from his coat pocket, emptied out a tablet, and chewed this although the directions said to suck. He was a martyr to his digestion. He was a martyr to many things, as the customary sour expression on his thin, elongated face suggested.

He walked along to the gate, opened it, stepped into the garden. He briefly looked at the narrow flowerbed full of colour, edged with small, fantastically shaped rocks, and thought that gardening was an awful waste of time; he went round to the front door, past the long, sloping roof, with its handmade peg-tiles which had been coloured by the centuries, and thought that people who lived in old houses and thereby suffered all the attendant discomforts, needed their brains examined. When the front door was opened, he regarded Kate with a disapproval that wasn't quite as hidden as he imagined; he believed that no matter how shapely, a woman should wear a skirt, not trousers. 'Mrs Stevens?'

'Yes.'

'I am Detective-Constable Ford.'

She responded to his pompously made announcement in typical fashion. 'So anything I say will be taken down and used in evidence?'

Lacking a developed sense of humour, he replied stiffly: 'I would like a word with you.'

'I imagine you have some means of identification?'

He showed her his warrant card, annoyed that she should have needed this to confirm him to be a man of authority.

'Come on in and tell me what's the trouble.'

Once they were in the sitting-room, she made an effort to be pleasant, despite his manner. 'Do sit down. Would you like some coffee?'

'Not for me.' His sympathies weren't that easily bought. 'You know Mr G. Weston who lives in London?'

'No.'

'According to what I've been told, you most certainly do.'

'Then I suggest you go back and tell your informant that I most certainly don't.'

'Why does Mr Weston say he knows you?'

She allowed her annoyance to show. 'I can hardly be expected to explain someone else's misapprehension.'

'He says he was in this house a week ago.'

'Then he has a remarkable imagination. I know no one by the name of Weston . . .' She stopped.

'Well?'

'I've just remembered. I'm afraid I'm being rather silly and completely forgetting something.'

'You're saying now that you do know him?'

'I've met him the once, last week.'

'Why did he come here?'

'To ask me . . .' She became silent.

'To ask you what?' he demanded roughly, believing her silence suggested a sense of guilt because he lacked the ability to realize it might express grief, too abruptly recalled.

'It was to ask me about my brother.'

'What about him?'

'I don't see that that is any concern of yours.'

He would have given a lot to tell her what he thought of her. 'How long have you known Mr Weston?'

'Last week was the only time I've ever met him and he was here for just a very short while—half an hour, maybe. In a social sense, I'd say I don't know him. Why are you asking?'

'His wife died last week.'

'Oh! . . . The poor man.'

'Did you know Mrs Weston?'

'I've obviously not made myself very clear. I've no idea what Mr Weston's circumstances are and so until now I've had no idea he was married.'

'You're quite certain you and he didn't have a bit of chat about her?'

'Are you deliberately misunderstanding me? If I'd no idea he was married, I could hardly have discussed his wife with him.'

'She died during that afternoon,' he said with deliberate crudeness. 'What time was he here?'

'I don't really know.'

'You must do.'

'If you have to have a time, I suppose it was somewhere between three-thirty and five.'

'Was anyone else present?'

'No. I live on my own.'

'Then you can't verify what you've told me?'

'I see no need to do so.'

'It might be in your interests, Mrs Stevens, since Mrs Weston's death may not have been an accident.'

'Are you trying to suggest something?' She stood. 'I think it's time you left.'

'I've not finished . . .'

'I have.'

He was not used to being dismissed; normally he dealt with people who had cause to be afraid of him and therefore took care not to offend him.

*

'She's certainly not my cup of tea,' said Ford spitefully.

Detective-Sergeant Feakin looked up. 'I don't remember asking if she was.' He resumed scraping out the bowl of his pipe with the small blade of a penknife. 'What's she say about Weston?'

'That she's only ever met him the once, last week, and then for no more than half an hour.'

'Did she give a time?'

'Between three-thirty and five and wouldn't get any more precise than that.'

Feakin put down the pipe and penknife, searched among the papers on his desk until he found the one he wanted. He read. 'The time of death is given as sixteen minutes past four.'

Ford said: 'She couldn't be certain of the time, but by pure chance she virtually gives him an alibi for the murder.'

'The request for the witness statement makes it perfectly clear that as yet there's no proof it was murder.' He looked up. 'I hope to God you didn't imply it was?'

'D'you think I'm wet behind the ears?'

'Just raw . . . Did she say why, if they'd never met before, he called there last week?'

'To talk about her brother.'

'What about him?'

'She refused to tell me.'

'What was her general attitude?'

'Aggressively rude.'

'Because of nerves?'

'Because she's a stuck-up bitch.'

Feakin tapped his pipe on an ashtray to eject the scrapings. Ford was normally a good interrogator; but occasionally he allowed resentment to cloud his judgement and failed to appreciate that a pleasant approach could be more appropriate and more likely to produce dividends. 'OK. Write up the report and I'll send it to London.'

'You can add that it's ten to one he's humping her as hard as he can go.'

'You're allowing envy to confuse the facts.'

CHAPTER 15

Kate, who did not like London and visited it as seldom as possible, finally managed to find Baston Common. She braked to a halt. The telephone directory had given the address and the name Francavilla had conjured up in her mind a retired colonial's dream house with sugar-plum towers; but it was clear that the common was ringed by blocks of flats and substantial houses of impeccably unimaginative taste.

She resumed driving, going round the common in a clock-wise direction so that she was on the side of the buildings and could more easily read the names or numbers. She found Francavilla and parked. It was the largest house she had passed, was set in the largest garden, and there was a Sierra outside the garage and a Mercedes inside. Clearly, there was considerable money here. The knowledge in-creased her fears because it made them more likely to be true. She wanted to turn and leave—until she was certain, she could always fool herself that her suspicions were ridicu-lous—but she had never run away. She squared her shoulders, opened the wrought-iron gate, went up the path into the ridiculous porch and rang the bell.

Mrs Amis opened the door. 'Yes?'

'Is Mr Weston in? If he is, I'd like a word with him.'

'You'd best come in and wait.'

She watched Mrs Amis climb the stairs, cross the landing and disappear, then visually examined the hall. She had an instinctive, rather than knowledgeable, appreciation of fine furniture and furnishings and she noted several good pieces—a Kashan carpet whose colours were strikingly rich, a display cabinet of near-perfect proportions which housed a collection of porcelain figurines, an intricately carved oak chest—which individually were attractive, but whose setting and juxtaposition were somehow wrong so that they failed to provide a satisfying whole.

Mrs Amis returned. 'He says to go into the sitting-room and he won't be long,' she said as she stepped down on to the parquet floor.

Nothing more was said, but it appeared to Kate that she was meant to follow Mrs Amis. They went through the drawing-room—almost the size of the whole of the cottage—and into the sitting-room beyond.

Mrs Amis left. Kate, once again criticizing the style of furnishing—with only a little colour, cleverly used, the room could have been warm and welcoming—went over to the nearer window and looked out. By London standards, the garden was large. At the far end a man was trimming the edges of the lawn with a machine. A daily woman, a gardener, a large house, set in extensive grounds . . .

'Good morning.'

She had not heard him enter the room and so his greeting startled her. She turned. He was not wearing any sign of mourning and his expression suggested strain but not grief. She said, for once observing convention: 'I was very sorry to hear your wife had died.'

He replied with equal formality. 'Thank you . . . How did you know?'

'A detective told me yesterday.'

'A detective? . . . Why should he have mentioned it?'

She said, her voice high: 'You lied to me last week.'

In turn, he ignored what she had said: 'Who was this detective? What did he want?'

'You lied about how the boat foundered. So when the

detective asked questions about you, I wondered if what had happened in Spain was connected with whatever had happened here and thought that maybe you'd lied about Jason being dead . . . Please, tell me, what's the truth? I don't care what's going on, I just want to know the truth about everything.'

He would have preferred to continue to lie, but could not ignore her appeal. He went over to the nearest chair and slumped down on it. 'I was on holiday in Restina and was sitting at an outside café table when Jason came up and called me by my school nickname. At first I didn't recognize him . . .'

Haltingly, and leaving out only the exact way in which he had been blackmailed into crewing *Cristina II*, he told her how they'd sailed eastwards until dark and had then altered course for Morocco.

'When that happened, what did you think was the purpose of the trip?'

'When I first . . . I reckoned . . . Does it really matter?'

'Yes,' she answered sharply.

'It surely had to be illegal and . . .'

'And what?'

'Well, I knew Morocco exported a lot of hashish . . .'

'You thought Jason was engaged in drug-smuggling?'

He nodded.

'Was he?'

'When I accused him of that, he was furious. Couldn't understand how I could be so stupid as to think him capable of such a thing.'

'What happened?'

'We picked up three men.'

'Who were they? Where were they going?'

'Back to Spain; to Restina. But apart from the fact that they were most probably Spaniards, I learned nothing about them.'

'Since they didn't travel by a normal route, they had to be illegals, didn't they?'

After a moment he nodded. 'Terrorists seemed the obvious conclusion, but . . .'

'But what?'

'Two of them didn't look capable of terrorizing a sick rabbit.'

'What about the third man?'

'He was younger and a different character. When Jason and I said we had to slow down and make for safety, he demanded we stayed on course at full cruising speed. He pulled a gun on us when we tried to refuse. Jason set out to overcome him, but failed, and was shot in the shoulder. I was at the helm . . .' He was silent for a moment. Then he continued. 'I did as ordered.' He'd called himself coward many times since, but had he really been one? Surely there had to be a choice for there to be cowardice?

'And then?'

'I edged as far to the north as I reckoned I could without alerting the man, to close the coast. The sea and swell increased and eventually caught me out and we were swept beam on. She broke up so quickly there wasn't time to launch the inflatable or even grab a life-jacket. I found myself in the water and completely by luck grabbed hold of something buoyant. It turned out that we'd approached very close to the coast and I was washed ashore. When the police questioned me, I said that Jason and I had been on a pleasure trip and had been caught in the storm. They decided we were just another couple of foreign, bloody fools, weekend seamen, and accepted what I'd told them.'

'Why did you come and see me last week?'

He showed his surprise at the question. 'To discover if you'd heard from Jason, of course.'

'Knowing he'd been shot in the shoulder so that one arm

was virtually incapacitated; that the odds were all against his surviving?'

'His body hadn't been recovered. I was hoping against hope.'

'Why didn't you tell me all this then?'

He spoke slowly. 'We'd obviously been engaged in something underhand and almost certainly illegal, though I'd no idea what. I didn't want you to know this because that's not the way to remember a brother.'

She spoke so quietly that he could only just catch her words. 'He was always wild. He was expelled from St Brede's, as you know, and that almost broke our parents' hearts; later on, Father had to pay several thousands of pounds to bail him out of trouble and that's when he finally washed his hands of him because he said Jason was rotten. I tried to persuade him Jason was wild, not wicked, but he wouldn't listen. He was so certain that Jason's behaviour was responsible for my mother's death. Jason and I were always close, even though we didn't see much of each other in later years; even after he'd been so beastly about Ben. But when you came and told me he was probably dead and you lied about the trip, I was terrified that he'd altered and had begun to do vicious things . . . But he hadn't. Just wild things.' She looked at him, her eyes moist. 'Can you forget the foul things I've said to you?'

'What foul things?'

They were quiet for a while, wrapped up in their own thoughts. He broke the silence. 'It was a detective who told you about Stephanie's death?'

She nodded.

'What was he doing at your place?'

'He'd somehow learned you'd called on the Wednesday and wanted to confirm the fact.'

'I told the police here where I was the afternoon

Stephanie died. God knows why that is of the slightest importance.'

She looked quickly at him and saw no suggestion of guile in his expression. So was he completely honest and therefore unable to appreciate their suspicions; or was he a possible murderer who was expert at concealing his true character? She prided herself on being able to judge a man's basic character. Even when she'd known him to be lying, she had been unable to escape her instinctive judgement that basically he was an honest man. Now, he had confirmed that judgement by explaining the reason for his lies. In her world, an honest man was incapable of murdering his wife, whatever the surrounding circumstances.

'If the police are making the kind of inquiries they are, it must mean they're not satisfied about something. D'you think your wife's death could have anything to do with what happened in Spain?'

'Of course it couldn't. Her death was an accident.'

She hesitated for a while, then said: 'The detective's manner seemed to suggest . . . well, that perhaps it wasn't an accident.'

'Then he's as stupid as the men up here, with all their questions about whether she had any enemies, how did she get the bruising on her stomach.'

'One of the things he wanted to know was if there was anyone who could verify that you were at Melton Cottage that afternoon.'

'So you told him that you could?'

'Yes, but . . .'

'Wouldn't he believe you?'

'He . . . made it clear he wanted the evidence of a third person because he thought we'd known each other for some time.'

'You must have set him right on that score very quickly?'

'I tried to, of course. But . . . I don't think he was prepared to believe me.'

'You're making it sound as if you're trying to tell me something?'

She took a deep breath. 'He was a ferrety man and I've hated ferrets ever since one bit me badly when I was ten. But I don't think it was just dislike which made it seem . . . that he was certain we were having an affair,' she ended in an embarrassed rush.

'Are you serious?'

'Can't you understand? The police think that perhaps you murdered your wife on account of me.'

He stared at her, initially with astonishment, then with a growing anger. 'Are you sick?'

'Of course I'm not.'

'Mentally sick, I mean.'

'What a filthy question.' Her embarrassment was very rapidly giving way to anger.

'You have to be badly disturbed to come here and say I murdered Stephanie because of you.'

'I said, that's what the detective believes.'

'You don't think that you have to be mentally disturbed to conceive such a possibility in him?'

'You bastard!' She stood.

'I'm sorry,' he said formally.

She hurried over to the door and had opened it by the time he was standing; when he reached there, she was already in the hall; as he entered the hall, she was slamming the front door shut behind herself.

As she walked rapidly towards her parked car, she suffered the humiliating certainty that in his mind she was a sex-starved woman, finding some sort of warped satisfaction by imagining that others believed they were having an affair.

CHAPTER 16

Detective-Inspector Rentlow read through the report as he stood by the window. 'Well?'

Waters answered briefly, knowing how much the DI disliked verbose or sloppy judgements. 'I'd call it short on facts and long on suppositions.'

The DI walked back to his desk, sat. 'I'd agree, always remembering that the only facts we have concerning the relationship are those that Weston and Mrs Stevens have provided so that one has to rely to some extent on suppositions. If she and Weston are waltzing on the mattress, it provides a strong motive for the murder.' He drummed on the desk with the fingers of his left hand. 'Has anyone talked to the mother to discover what she has to say about the marriage?'

'Not yet.'

'You'd better arrange that. And find out if anyone saw Weston near the house at around the time of his wife's death.'

Somewhat unwisely, Waters raised an objection. 'That's going to tie up a lot of manpower when we aren't even yet sure we're dealing with a murder.'

'Can you suggest a way of becoming sure without making further inquiries?' the DI asked sarcastically. The Detective-Sergeant's plodding attitude might have its advantages, but there were times when it annoyed him.

There was a knock on the door. The DI called out to enter, but did not immediately look up. When he did, he saw a PC. 'Yes?'

'There's a report just in for you, sir; a car was coming

down from County HQ and they brought it.' He passed across a rectangular brown envelope.

As he slit open the envelope, the PC left. Inside was the pathologist's full report on the post-mortem of Stephanie Weston. It proved to be far more precise than he had expected. The deceased had been in good physical condition for her age and there was no apparent reason for her to have suffered any unexpected loss of balance such as would result from an unexpected attack of dizziness. There was bruising behind the voice-box and a hairline fracture of the cornu. It could be said, without fear of contradiction, that both had been caused by pressure—from fingers, not a ligature—applied to the throat; pressure then relaxed so that the victim had not been killed. A feasible interpretation of events was that an attempt had been made either to frighten or actually to strangle the victim; in her panic, she had managed to escape her assailant and had run for safety, but had cannoned into something—the banisters?— had fallen and had suffered fatal injuries to her head.

He put the report down on his desk. So now they knew that it was a case of either murder or manslaughter.

Had she been a sensible woman, Monica Badger would have moved into a much smaller house; but a large one impressed, while a small one did not. Dressed in unrelieved black, she showed the PC into the drawing-room. A length of black satin ribbon had been draped over the silver-framed photograph of her daughter on the mantelpiece.

'Just a question or two,' said the PC, before he sat uneasily on a chair with thin, bowed legs which made him worried that it might not take his weight. He held his pencil and notebook at the ready. Recently seconded to the CID as aide, he was still very keen and conscientious. 'Like I said, it's on account of you having said your daughter was maybe murdered.'

'Not maybe; was murdered.' Age had not been kind to Monica since it had imprinted sour discontent on her face. She spoke at length, letting her sorrowing hatred spill out.

At first the PC made voluminous notes, but when she began to repeat herself he only went through the motions. There would surely, he thought, have been more satisfaction to be gained from murdering the mother rather than the daughter. When she repeated herself for the third time, he risked interrupting her. 'I suppose she talked to you a lot?'

'She always confided in me; we were more like two sisters than mother and daughter. And when she discovered what sort of a man he really was . . .'

'So what kind was that?'

'A fortune-seeker. That's what I told her when she first became infatuated by his clever tongue, but she wouldn't listen. I knew something terrible was going to happen.' She brushed her eyes with a lace-edged handkerchief.

'You're saying she had money of her own?'

'My husband left her a fortune.'

'You wouldn't like to say roughly how much?'

'I have no idea,' she replied sharply, rebuking him for his impertinence.

'D'you know what happens to it now?'

'He insisted on making a will in which he left her everything he possessed, so she did the same, naming just him. I tried to warn her that as he hadn't anything to leave, his was a meaningless gesture designed to show good faith and to trick her into reciprocating. She wouldn't believe me. She simply wouldn't see the truth about him.'

'How did things go for them?'

'I don't understand.'

'Did they get on well together, despite the problems?'

'She made herself a slave. Even when she began to understand what he was really like, her one desire was to make him happy.' She warmed to the theme. Stephanie had been the dutiful, long-suffering wife who had tried to reach his heart with love; he had rejected her with brutal cynicism, interested only in gaining her fortune.

'Did she give him money from time to time?'

'He had so poor a job, she had to. She bought the house and paid all the running expenses. And not even that was enough for him, so he was forever trying to persuade her to let him manage her affairs.'

'But she refused?'

'I told her over and over again that if she did that, he'd rob her blind.'

'When's the last time he was on to her to let him handle her money?'

'At the beginning of this year. And you know why he was so eager, don't you?'

'Can't say I do, Mrs Badger.'

'He wanted to steal as much of her money as he could before going off with another woman.'

'You're saying he had a girlfriend?'

'That kind of man always does.' Her voice was harsh. She was remembering the day she discovered that her husband rented a flat in the next town in which a young woman half his age offered him the pleasures that any decent woman refused.

'Can you give me the lady's name and address?'

'I have no idea what they are.'

'Your daughter told you about her but didn't give any details?'

'Like me, she knew there was someone, but no more than that because he is a cunning man. It hurt her more than anyone but a mother can ever appreciate . . .'

Twenty minutes later the PC returned to his car, lit a cigarette, and wondered whether marriage was all it was cracked up to be.

*

Turner took a handkerchief from his trouser pocket and mopped the sweat from his forehead. It was weather to make a man dream of Mediterranean beaches. The previous night he'd tentatively suggested to Pauline that they went on holiday to Greece—no hint of a double room, of course. She hadn't said yes, but then she hadn't said no. Just so long as that bastard with a Morgan didn't flourish a fortnight in the Seychelles . . .

He crossed the forecourt of the block of flats to the front door. There was an entryphone with eight nameplates and eight buttons. He pressed the first, but there was no reply; he pressed the second and a deep, female voice asked him what he wanted. He identified himself. The door buzzed and he went in. There was a lift but it was at the top floor so he climbed the stairs and thought that people who lived in these luxurious flats probably weren't aware that one could go on holiday this side of the Pacific.

The woman who let him into Flat No. 2 had a very heavily featured face devoid of any make-up, a lumpy and unsupported body, wore a man's shirt, tie, and slacks, and was smoking a pipe. But he was broad-minded. He asked her if she knew the Westons who lived in Francavilla. She replied that she'd always taken great care not to know anyone who lived in a house with a bloody silly name.

Flat 3 was occupied by an elderly couple. They told him they'd only moved in in the past month, having sold their country home because they'd found it too difficult to manage there any longer. It was a nice flat, but there were people in one of the top ones who would leave the doors of the lift open so that no one else could use it; as he was a policeman, would he ask them to close it always? And no, they'd never met the Westons.

In Flat 4 he met two middle-aged women. Mrs Edwardes introduced her friend, Mrs Ackroyd, then said that her husband was at work, but of course she'd help if she could. First, however, would he like a drink? He chose orange juice.

Mrs Edwardes settled on one of the chairs. She knew the Westons; just casually, a now-and-then kind of a friendship, was how she described it. Why was the detective-constable interested?

Glass of orange juice in hand, he explained. There was some evidence which pointed to the possibility that on the afternoon Mrs Weston had so tragically died, there had been a visitor to the house. If this were so, the police would like to contact that person to find out if he, or she, could help in any way to resolve the question of why Mrs Weston had had the accident.

'But surely there wasn't anything unusual about it?' Mrs Edwardes asked.

'I don't think so, no. But almost all fatal accidents are investigated and analysed these days.'

'I see.' But clearly she did not and was puzzled. 'I'm sorry, but I'm not certain what day the accident was on?'

'A week ago, last Wednesday. As far as we can tell, between three and five in the afternoon.'

She thought for a moment. 'That's the day I had to go up to the City because Charles's firm was having a luncheon to which all wives were commanded to appear on pain of excommunication.' She turned and spoke to Mrs Ackroyd. 'I didn't return until well after five, did I?'

'I'd have said it was nearer six.'

'I suppose it must have been. It was your first day here and I was so annoyed at having to sit and listen to the risqué, after-dinner jokes of a chairman who's never mentally matured beyond the fifth form.' She faced Turner once more. 'I'm sorry, but I won't be able to help you.'

'Thanks anyway.' He drained his glass, put it down.

'Just a minute,' said Mrs Ackroyd. 'I went for a walk in

the afternoon and I might have seen someone. Exactly which house is it you're talking about?'

'About five places along from here,' answered Turner.

'It's the largest house left on the common,' said Mrs Edwardes. 'There's a weeping pear tree in the corner of the front garden.'

'And it has a ridiculous porch?'

'That's right, but it's a good job Stephanie can't hear you say that. She was very proud of her "classical" entrance.'

'Architectural glaucoma.' Mrs Ackroyd picked up her handbag from the side of the chair on which she was sitting. 'Does anyone mind if I smoke?'

'I do,' replied Mrs Edwardes immediately, 'but that's not stopped you in the past.'

'I can remember so much more clearly when I'm smoking.'

'That really is the most fatuous excuse I've ever heard!'

Smiling, Mrs Ackroyd offered Turner a cigarette. He thanked her, refused. She lit one with a slim gold lighter. 'I remember looking at my watch and deciding I'd better get back as it was just before four and I thought my hostess would be returning soon. I came along on the common side of the road and then stopped because I noted a weeping pear tree and one doesn't see them all that often. That's when I noticed the porch. I must say, it's difficult to imagine anyone being proud of something quite so pretentious.'

'While you were looking at the house, did you notice anyone around it?' Turner asked.

She drew on the cigarette, let the smoke trickle out of her nostrils. 'As a matter of fact, I did.'

'Who?'

'While I was still staring, two men came round from the side of the house, out on to the pavement, and walked away. I thought at the time . . .' She became silent.

'Yes, Mrs Ackroyd?'

'Look, I know how easy it is to imagine something when you know there's reason to. But at the time I really did notice that they seemed to be in a hurry . . . Perhaps they wanted to call for help for Mrs Weston?'

'They'd have used the phone,' said Mrs Edwardes.

'Of course! How stupid of me.'

'Vera's an artist,' Mrs Edwardes said to Turner.

He wasn't certain how that was meant to affect his judgement of the evidence. He asked Mrs Ackroyd: 'You're positive it was the house with the pear tree and the big porch?'

'Weeping pear tree. There's a tremendous difference, you know. Yes, I am quite positive. And there's another thing I've just remembered. I saw them get into a car and drive off very quickly and recklessly; they never looked to see if another car was coming up behind and there was very nearly a bad accident.'

'Can you describe them?'

'I'm not certain. I mean, they were the other side of the road, there was quite a lot of traffic, and in any case I can't say I was all that interested in what they looked like.'

'But as an artist, you must have some sort of mental picture of them?'

Mrs Edwardes laughed. 'Vera's a botanical artist, not a portrait-painter. If it had been an example of a rare pterido-phyte, she'd be able to draw every frond down to the last minute detail.'

He said that he knew it was difficult to describe another person, but would Mrs Ackroyd try?

Both men had been wearing caps—baseball caps, she believed they were called—with large peaks, and dark glasses which obscured much of their faces. Both had been roughly of the same age, in their late twenties or early thirties; both had worn what had looked like golf jackets and jeans. The one on the inside had never been readily visible so she could only add that he had had a square rather than an oval face. The one on the outside had had the smooth, hungry looks which she always associated with Latin-American gigolos; although she had gained the impression that there was a toughness to his character which meant he was far from being a gigolo. But beyond that, she was afraid she couldn't help . . .

'You've done better than usual,' he said.

'Really?' She was gratified.

'About the car they drove off in—have you any idea what make it was?'

'These days they all look the same to me.'

'What sort of colour?'

She thought, then said uncertainly: 'Probably light grey or blue.'

'And I don't suppose you noticed any details about the number plate?'

'None at all.'

There was nothing more of any consequence that she could tell him. It had been a casual incident, only casually observed.

'Two men?' said Waters.

'That's the way she tells it,' replied Turner.

'Maybe she's talking about a different day?'

'She was very definite it was Wednesday. And Mrs Edwardes confirmed that by saying she was away in the afternoon at a big nosh-up in the City.'

'But two men?'

'He's squeamish and took a pal along to do the dirty work.'

'A contract job, with him going along to lead the way and open up the house with a key so there are no signs of forced entry? And to say, it's only hubby, no need to be alarmed.'

'Why not?'

'He'd have to be a right nasty bastard to be that cold-blooded.'

'With a fortune and a nice bit of bed-warmer waiting, why not?'

'Don't ever ask me for a moral reference . . . We've heard from Crosford. Mrs Badger claims Weston only married her daughter for the money, was always trying to get her to let him manage her financial affairs, named him her sole beneficiary, and the marriage was a failure.'

'It all fits, as neat as an Eskimo in an igloo.' Turner settled on the desk. 'Everything is working.'

'Which is more than you're doing right now. Organize an identification session on the computer with Mrs Ackroyd and see if she comes up with a likeness of Weston.'

Turner slid off the desk and began to cross to the door.

'One quid gives you four that you can't tell me what colour Weston's two cars are,' Waters said.

'The Mercedes is dark blue and the Sierra is a light fawn. Where's the four quid?'

'Up your jack-staff,' replied Waters crudely.

'There are a lot of trees lining the edge of the common,' said Turner.

'So?'

'They create shadows and with a speckled pattern it's not always easy to tell true colour. Light fawn could easily look like light blue or grey.'

'If you're not careful, you'll soon con yourself into believing you actually saw him do it.'

Kate knelt on an old cushion and used a trowel to scrape out a little more earth, then again set the stone down in the hole; this time, all was well and she packed the loose earth around its base as tightly as she could. These stones, bordering the narrow flowerbed, were magical; every now and then one of them moved and clearly only magical ones could do that. Early in her marriage, she'd found them on the shore, under some cliffs, and had been so intrigued by their extraordinary shapes and surfaces—spiky, holey, cavernous; a witch's gruyère cheese—that she'd insisted several times on bringing back as many as the boot of the car would hold. Each time Keith had jeered at her for being so stupid; he was a man who seldom saw beauty in anything that wasn't smoothly normal. Perhaps it was because of his scorn that she now invested any movement with magical origins and not because a mole had burrowed nearby, heavy rain had washed away supporting earth, or the edge of the mower had knocked a stone. A belief in magic could help to soothe a mental scar.

She heard a car drive in and stop. Unable to see who was the caller because of the thorn hedge, she stood. A tall, thin, angular woman, dressed in a flowing print frock, waved. Kate sighed.

'I've brought you the parish magazine,' Miss Hammond said in her carefully articulated voice as she walked through the gateway.

'That's very kind of you. D'you have time for a cup of tea?' Kate had always allowed compassion to override her true wishes; not even marriage to Keith had cured her of that weakness.

'I shouldn't, because I've several other homes to visit . . . But I suppose perhaps I could play hookey for a little.' She often spoke as if her schooldays were just behind her rather than clear out of sight.

They went into the house. Miss Hammond settled in the sitting-room, Kate carried on through to the kitchen where she switched on the kettle, put some chocolate biscuits on a tray along with cups, saucers, teaspoons, sugar, milk, and a strainer, and wondered whether her guest would leave before the television programme on the Galapagos started on BBC 2.

During tea, Miss Hammond provided her customary quota of gossip and misinformation. The vicar had upset many of his parishioners by his wish to limit the number of flowers in church; the butcher from the next village had been caught trying to sell meat which should have been condemned; the daughter of the family who owned the manor had ... She related the highly scandalous story in such prurient detail that Kate wondered if she really understood what she was saying.

'And then, of course, you've had your own little excitement!'

Kate nibbled a biscuit. 'Have I?'

'That attempted burglary.'

'What attempted burglary?'

'I understand. Unless it's happened to oneself, one cannot begin to appreciate how upsetting it can be. I always remember how in the old days when one travelled by ship, the Customs used to make one open every single suitcase and go through it, fingering one's clothes. I always felt as if I'd been defiled.'

Had she really felt a loss of virginity when her underclothes were touched by a Customs officer?

'So of course, dear, you're reluctant to talk about it. But as I always say, a trouble shared is a trouble halved. Did the beastly men actually get inside?'

'I'm sorry, but I just don't know what you're talking about.'

Her face quivered with excitement; so flat a denial suggested dark undercurrents. 'Mavis was asked about it by the detective.'

'Asked about what?'

'Whether she'd seen any strange men near your house in the past few weeks.'

Mavis lived at the end of the road. She always complained of having too much to do to have any time to herself, but as a fount of information concerning the comings and goings of the local inhabitants she was the equal of Miss Hammond. 'Why should a detective want to know that?'

'Because of the attempted burglary, of course. The police are trying to discover if anyone saw the burglars.'

'You're saying that a detective has been asking if any strangers have been seen near here because of an attempted burglary?'

'That's right.'

'What a load of absolute rubbish!'

Miss Hammond left forty-seven minutes later, piqued that Kate refused to discuss the matter in detail.

Kate carried the tray through to the kitchen, put the dirty things on the draining-board, and nibbled the remaining biscuit as she walked to the sitting-room. She sat, checked the time and saw there was still a quarter of an hour before the programme she wanted to watch, stared into space. Since there'd been no attempted burglary, either Miss Hammond had the story even more wrong that usual or the detective had been talking nonsense. Miss Hammond often did get her facts muddled, but in this case Kate was prepared to believe that she had not. Policemen normally never talked nonsense. So the only logical explanation of the story was that the detective had been making inquiries about the identities of her legitimate visitors while trying to conceal that fact. In other words, he'd been trying to discover if Weston was a frequent visitor; frequent enough to make it obvious that he was her lover. Because if so, then he might well have decided to get rid of his wife in order to marry her . . .

She thought she must warn him. But then she remembered how their previous meeting had ended and she decided that he could damn well find out the hard way.

CHAPTER 17

Mrs Amis lived in north Baston, only a mile from Baston Common but an area that was totally different in character. Here, there were no large Edwardian houses or blocks of luxurious flats, only council estates and streets of downmarket semi-detacheds or terrace houses. Her daughter had married and now lived in Carlisle and seldom came south; she was on her own for most of the time.

She was making tea when the doorbell chimed. She left the kitchen and went along the short passage to the front door.

'Hullo,' said Turner.

She studied him. 'What d'you want?' Her abrupt manner was seldom intended to be as rude as it sounded.

'I'd like a word if you've the time.'

'And what if I haven't?'

He grinned.

'I suppose you'd best come in.' She showed him into the front room, looking as if it had been spring-cleaned only that morning. 'I'm making a cuppa. D'you fancy one?'

'No need to ask twice.'

She brought the tea in, handed him a mug and told him to help himself to milk and sugar, sat with a sigh which suggested tired or rheumaticky limbs. 'So why d'you want a word? Because it wasn't no accident?'

'What makes you ask that?'

'Because coppers don't go around asking questions when there's no need.'

'We always have to check the facts surrounding fatal accidents.'

'Since when?'

'Since we were told we had to . . . What I'd like to hear is who's called at Francavilla recently.'

'I only work mornings.'

'Yeah, I know that.'

She thought, mentioned some names, paused, added a few more; to a couple she appended sharp, critical comments on character.

'Were they her friends or his, or both?'

'Mostly hers. I mean, he was at work in the mornings until he was given the push, wasn't he, so who'd be calling to see him?'

'Either before or after her death, did you ever see a woman in her middle twenties with red hair; not bad-looking, probably.'

'I can't see what it's got to do with you.'

'Suppose you leave me to work that out. You have seen one such, haven't you? When?'

She had an old-fashioned respect for the law. 'I suppose it were last week.'

'And I'm betting she was still there when you left.'

'Then you've lost your bet.'

'Maybe she went out to do a bit of shopping for lunch?'

'She left because they had a row.'

'How would you know that?'

'They was talking so loud I could tell they was arguing, even if I couldn't understand the words. And when she left, she slammed the front door like she wanted to knock the house down.'

Why should they have had a row? Because he'd refused to marry her in the immediate future, on the grounds that it would be too dangerous to do so?

*

Compiling the computerized image of a person from a description was a long, arduous, and very often frustrating task which was why Waters—at home with a keyboard and a VDU, unlike so many policemen—usually carried it out. His placid acceptance of repeated failures and his optimistic certainty that the next attempt would bring success helped many a witness to persevere.

He asked Mrs Ackroyd to describe in general terms the face of the man she had seen the more clearly. She did so. He brought standard shapes on screen, altered them, and discarded them as she criticized what she saw. After twenty minutes she said wearily that it was hopeless.

He suggested a break and a smoke. They discussed gardening, in particular the latest varieties of floribunda which, it was claimed, had a strong scent, and it was over a quarter of an hour before he turned back to the computer. This time he had a little more success. After many slight alterations to the third image, she said that this was certainly the nearest they'd got, although it still wasn't good. He printed it out. He asked her if she'd have a shot at reproducing the face of the second man, but she refused on the grounds that she had seen him so much less clearly than his companion and it was only a very poor likeness of the latter which they'd managed to produce.

He thanked her for her help, accompanied her down to the main entrance, then returned to the computer room and picked up the printout. He took this through to the CID general room and showed it to Turner. 'Does this ring any bells?'

'Only alarm ones. Looks like he'd cut your guts out with a penknife for laughs.'

'Witnesses usually look on the black side of people. You can't see any resemblance to Weston?'

'None at all. So either this is the second man or her memory has more holes than a colander.'

'Or neither man was Weston.'
'And the average MP is honest.'

The day was overcast, the air moist, and Mrs Amis wore an old raincoat on her walk from the bus stop to Francavilla. She unlocked the service back door and entered, went from the passage into the utility room where she hung up her raincoat, and put on an apron. In the kitchen, the dirty luncheon, supper, and breakfast things had all been put in the dishwasher, the butter and milk returned to the refrigerator and jams and condiments to the cupboards, and the pots and coffee-maker stacked neatly on the right-hand draining-board. Had Stephanie still been alive, everything would have been left in confusion on the table or in the dining- and breakfast-rooms.

She washed up the pots and coffee-maker, then collected the vacuum cleaner and went through to the library. She had a great respect for learning, though not necessarily for those who were learned, and viewed the hundreds of books, many bound in leather, with a degree of awe.

She had just finished vacuuming the floor when Weston entered.

''Morning, Mr W.' She liked him because he was always polite and friendly, never showing a hint of the condescension which his wife had. She agreed with her late husband; money didn't make a man better, just richer.

'I won't interrupt you for long. There's just a paper I need.' He went round his desk and opened the top right-hand drawer.

'I had a visitor yesterday afternoon,' she said.

He brought out a sheet of paper, slid the drawer shut, waited.

'It were the detective what's been here a time or two.'

'What did he want?'

She was sorry that the news obviously disturbed him.

'He was being real nosey. Asking what visitors had been here, especially a young lady with red hair.'

'What about her?'

'Like I said, he was asking if she'd called.'

'What did you say?'

'I had to tell him, didn't I?'

'I suppose so ... Yes, of course you did. Could you understand why he was asking about her?'

'He didn't say nothing except he bet she stayed on after I left. I told him, he wasn't as smart as he thought.'

'I guess that would be rather difficult,' he said. He tried to dismiss the episode as meaningless, but couldn't.

The telephone rang and since Weston had not brought the cordless receiver into the sitting-room, he went into the hall to answer the call.

'It's Eleanor. How are things, Gary?'

'Not too bad, all things considered.' He liked both the Edwardes, but Stephanie had found Eleanor too sharp and self-opinionated.

'The moment you feel you want to see people again, will you come and have a meal with us?'

'That's very kind.'

'I'm not going to make a definite date because you'll know when to socialize. When my sister lost her husband, she threw herself into an outside life; when a friend of ours lost his wife, by choice he became a virtual recluse. So it's entirely up to you. But you must promise to get in touch the moment you want a change.'

'I promise, with hand on heart.'

'Good ... I suppose you know the police are making inquiries?'

'Yes.'

'Without wishing to be a prying Pauline, is there some query about the accident?'

Stephanie would have said that only a woman of Eleanor's insensitivity could have asked the question so directly. 'They seem to think there may be, though God knows why. How have you heard about it?'

'A detective was here on Saturday, questioning people in all the flats.'

'What kind of questioning?'

'He said there might have been a caller at your house on the Wednesday and wondered if anyone had seen this man. He was a perfectly pleasant person, but rather sly I would say. Still, I suppose one has to be sly to be a good detective. I told him I couldn't help since I was in London that afternoon. I had to go to a simply excruciating lunch with Charles; as always, the food was cardboard, the wine sour, and the speeches mind-numbing. Worse still, it was non-tax-deductible.'

'What man do they think might have called?'

'I don't know, really, but Vera may have seen them. She's been staying with us and was out for a walk in the afternoon and saw two men come away from your place and drive off in a hurry. The police asked her to go to the station and to sit down in front of a computer to try to construct a likeness.'

'Did she succeed?'

'Not really. Unless you can draw, it really is almost impossible to describe another person, isn't it? ... Well, I must get a move on and go and do some shopping. Charles demands a cooked meal every evening even though he's developing a pregnant tum ... Don't forget, you'll let me know as soon as you feel like some company.'

He replaced the receiver. Who were the two men? Stephanie could not have been expecting anyone to call since she'd driven up to her mother's in the morning and would not have known when she'd be back ...

CHAPTER 18

The Detective-Inspector looked at the computer portrait. 'It seems we're going to have to forget eye-witness identification.'

'Why, sir?' asked Turner.

Waters briefly looked up at the ceiling.

'You don't think that this is rather useless?' asked Rentlow sarcastically, tapping the portrait.

Unlike Waters, Turner was prepared to argue a case when it was obvious that a senior regarded it as beyond argument. 'As I understand it, Mrs Ackroyd says it's not a good likeness.'

'So?'

'So before giving up, shouldn't we get a photo of Weston and show her that?'

'Why?'

'Because the evidence says that one of the men must have been him.'

'Evidence? If there's any of that around, no one's bothered to pass it on to me. All I've ever been given are suppositions.' Rentlow made a habit of acting as devil's advocate in order to force investigating detectives to sharpen their minds, but his present criticisms were due mainly to angry annoyance. This was the kind of case that was poison to an ambitious DI. Decide to drop it on the grounds that there was not enough evidence to go to court and he could be accused of lack of initiative; pursue it and fail to persuade a court to bring in a verdict of guilty and he could be accused of incompetence.

Turner said: 'His girlfriend's visited him after the wife's

death and one such visit ended in a row. That tells us how the land lies.'

'You must have thirty-thirty vision.'

'Look, sir, it locks everything in place. At the start, he's living with a wife who has the ready, buckets and buckets of it, but never loses a chance to remind him it's all hers; it's her house and she pays for the running of it while his salary, when he earns one, hardly keeps the cleaning lady happy. On top of that, he's frustrated something fierce because she reckons one goes to bed to sleep. Enter a red-head who gives him nookie like he's only ever dreamed about before; she thinks all the lovely money is his, so once she's got him hooked, she says she wouldn't mind marriage. But get shot of his wife and the money's gone and all he has left is what he can earn. Still, he's naïve because it's true love and everything will work out all right. That is, until he loses his job and he can't even give his girlfriend a box of Milk Tray. She makes one thing crystal clear—no diamond marriage, no more nookie. So he's only one move left. Murder the wife and make it look like an accident. The row was because she's in a hurry to try Mrs on for size, he realizes that if he openly shacks up too quickly, people— especially us—are going to wonder.'

'Put all that on paper and find the right publisher and you'll make a fortune.'

'That's the way it was, sir.'

'Explain one thing. How can you be so certain the girl-friend is that hot and willing?'

'She's got red hair.'

'And you call yourself a detective?'

'I once knew a redhead who taught me . . .'

'I'd rather not know the extent of your studies.' The DI stared at the computer portrait. 'You want to organize a photographic session and then show the photo to Mrs Ackroyd?'

'Yes, sir. And also to tackle him head on and question him hard. And make the questions personal because he's the kind of man who'll become really embarrassed by them and that'll knock him off balance.'

'I suppose it's either that or wait for something to break,' said Rentlow slowly.

The van was parked in Trefoil Road, on the side of the common, almost opposite Francavilla. On both of its black sides was a colourful and complicated logo, designed not to draw attention to the firm whose name was immediately below it—the firm did not exist—but to hide the two apertures in the centre.

Inside the van the photographer sweated and the PC, who was keeping a look-out through the smaller aperture, cursed his misfortune in landing a surveillance job because he'd been fool enough to admit that he knew Weston by sight. Hadn't four years' service been enough to teach him the prime rules of survival? Never volunteer . . . He saw the man step out from the shadow of the porch. A couple of cars passed before he was able to make an identification. 'He's surfaced.'

'About bloody time,' said the photographer. 'I feel like I'm about to dribble out through a crack in the floor.' He came to a kneeling position, picked up a camera with a telephoto lense, slid open the larger observation aperture. 'That's him, just coming up to the garden gate?'

'Right.'

'Here we go.' He took four photographs. 'That should do it. Always provided, of course, that I remembered to remove the dust cover.'

Weston left the Sierra—he had not driven the Mercedes since Stephanie had died—in the council car park and walked the short distance, past the vicarage, to the modern ten-storey concrete and glass divisional police HQ. A wide spiral ramp took him up to the first floor and the front room.

There were a sergeant and a PC behind the counter and the PC moved along to where he stood. He said he had an appointment with Detective-Sergeant Waters; he was asked to wait.

He sat on one of the chairs, picked up a magazine from the table and leafed through it, but put it down when he realized that he was not taking in even the photographs. Did everyone feel so disturbed when summoned for an interview by the police? Much surely must depend on guilt or innocence? Since he was innocent, he had absolutely no cause for apprehension . . .

Turner walked through one of the doorways, looked around and saw him, came across. ''Morning, Mr Weston. Kind of you to come along.'

Sarcasm? He thought so, but couldn't be certain.

'Would you like to follow me?'

Now, he was reminded of the corridor which had lead to the headmaster's study at St Brede's . . .

They entered a square, high-ceilinged room whose small, single window was barred. There was a table, around which were several wooden chairs and on which were a beaker of water, three glasses, several sheets of paper, and two pens. He was introduced to Waters. They sat.

'There are one or two things we want to clear up . . .' began Turner.

He interrupted. 'And there's something I mean to get straight. My wife died in an accident. Yet you lot are asking endless questions about my marriage, my wife, and me. What right have you to invade and insult my private life like that?'

'Every right, Mr Weston,' answered Waters quietly. 'You see, we've received the full report on the post-mortem and

I'm sorry to have to tell you that that establishes beyond any doubt that your wife did not die in an accident, but she was the victim of a constructive murder.'

'Oh Christ!' After a while he said hoarsely: 'What's a constructive murder?'

'It's the non-legal term we use when an assailant doesn't actually kill the victim, but his actions are directly responsible for the death. As far as we can reconstruct events, an intruder was attacking your wife. She managed to break free and ran at full speed across the landing and into the banisters; the force with which she did this caused her to overbalance.'

All too clearly, he could gauge her blind panic. It would have stripped her of all reason.

'Two men were seen leaving the grounds of the house at about the time of her death. They were in a hurry.'

'They killed her?'

'It seems likely they were responsible.'

'Why? What were they after? Did they think the house was empty, but found her there?'

'Casual thieves aren't experts and when they break into a house they leave plenty of traces, but there weren't any,' said Turner aggressively. 'Another thing, the Mercedes was in the garage to say that probably there was someone inside; casuals don't try a house that looks occupied.'

'Who else could it have been?'

'Two men who knew she was in the house.'

'Are you saying they meant to kill her? How many more times do I have to tell you that that's impossible?'

'We'd like to discover if that's right. So let's start by you telling us what kind of a marriage it was?'

Weston's astonishment was obvious; his anger only when he spoke. 'That's none of your goddamn business.'

Waters spoke quietly, in marked contrast to Turner. 'I'm sorry we need to ask, Mr Weston, because I can understand how you feel. But we really do have to know all the facts so that we can sort out what's important and what isn't.'

'This isn't.'

'It wasn't a happy marriage, was it?' said Turner.

'It was perfectly happy.'

'Mrs Badger denies that. She even went so far as to accuse you of the murder.'

'Of course she did.'

'Why d'you say "of course"?'

'Because she ... It's impossible to explain.'

'Mr Weston,' said Waters, 'once we know and can understand all the relationships involved, then we can decide in which direction we're most likely to find the murderer.'

He hesitated, then finally spoke, unwillingly and haltingly. The Badgers' marriage had been unhappy almost from the start because it would have been difficult to find two people more dissimilar in character. Finally, Andrew Badger had asked for a divorce, but she had refused to give him one; in those days there had been no divorce by mutual consent, only divorce through a partner's specific misbehaviour or prolonged mental instability, so if the aggrieved person chose not to bring an action, that was that. Andrew Badger had gained his revenge, but only after his death. A very wealthy man, he had left his wife only a tithe of his estate; and to ensure that she did not pursue a claim for a much greater part, he had set down on paper a long and detailed account of her physical and mental frigidity and had given instructions that this was to be produced in evidence in court should she ever make such a claim. He had understood his wife far better than she had understood him—nothing would persuade her ever to allow such evidence to become public. So she had accepted her relatively parsimonious legacy and had hated him even more dead than when alive.

People's emotions were seldom wholly logical. Her

hatred for her husband had become a hatred of all men. When she'd first been introduced to Weston, she'd been perfectly polite but reserved; only later had he understood that her reserved manner concealed not an initial, reasonable wait-and-see, but an immediate and unreasonable hatred. She had done everything she could to stop the wedding by poisoning Stephanie's mind against him, but Stephanie had had the kind of character which pulled ever harder in the opposite direction to that in which someone was trying to lead it. From the day of the marriage, she had never lost a chance to suggest that it was a failure; that he had married only for money; that he was having an affair with some other woman . . .

'So when I told her Stephanie had had a fatal accident, it was inevitable that she'd accuse me of murdering her.'

'For no reason whatsover?' asked Turner disbelievingly.

'For all the reasons I've just given.'

'It seems pretty far-fetched to suggest she'd accuse you of murder just because she and her old man hadn't seen eye-to-eye.'

'It'll only seem far-fetched to someone who doesn't understand human nature.'

'And you reckon to know all about it?'

Waters said quietly: 'So Mrs Badger is wrong when she claims that your marriage wasn't a happy one?'

'Yes,' replied Weston.

Turner was not prepared to stay silent for very long. 'So why did you go off to Spain on your own?'

'Why not?'

'All the husbands I know take their wives. Unless there's good reason, like a hot bim waiting on the sand.'

'Sorry to disappoint you, but I did not have a hot bim waiting—assuming that means a woman.'

'I know a couple who always take separate holidays,' said Waters. 'They reckon it's good for both of 'em to have a complete break. Maybe you and Mrs Weston were like that?'

Stephanie and he had not taken separate holidays before; a fact which could readily be ascertained. 'The reason why I went on my own is that we'd decided to take a holiday together in the early part of September to either Canada or South Africa. Then I was made redundant. I felt . . . Well, I couldn't afford the kind of holiday we'd planned, but I had to get away from everything. My wife did not want to go with me.'

'Whereabouts in Spain did you go?' Turner asked.

'Restina; that's on the Costa del Sol.'

'What was the name of the hotel.'

'Bahia Azul.'

'Why wouldn't Mrs Weston go with you?'

'Does that really matter?'

'Can't say until you tell us.'

'She disliked package holidays.'

'Because of all the erks and narks that use 'em?'

'Pack that in,' said Waters sharply.

Turner was unabashed. 'So if she didn't want to go slumming, why didn't you do as you were going to and try Canada or South Africa?'

'I've already explained, I couldn't afford that kind of a holiday any longer.'

'But she'd more than enough of the necessary.'

'Don't you understand a thing?'

'Suppose you help me by explaining?'

'I've always paid my own way.'

'Yeah? Then you shelled out half what your house cost? Or d'you mean you insisted on buying half the peanuts?'

'I said, knock it off,' snapped Waters, managing to sound annoyed by Turner's brash manner. 'Mr Weston, all we're trying to do is sort out things. You liked to pay your own way, your wife didn't like crowds, so you went on your own to Spain for the break. Did you meet anyone there by prior arrangement?'

'No.'

'Then we don't need to waste any more time . . . Now, I'd like to have a word about Wednesday, the twelfth. I believe that on that day you drove down to Kent to speak to Mrs Stevens?'

'Yes.'

'She's a friend?'

'I didn't know her before that day.'

Turner said: 'Then why did you want to see her?'

'I've also answered that before. I had to tell her that her brother was probably dead.'

'Probably? Why not a yes or a no?'

'Our boat foundered in a storm.'

'You survived. Why shouldn't he have done the same?'

He couldn't admit that Farley had been shot in the shoulder. 'He wasn't a good swimmer.'

'Weren't there any life-jackets or life-rafts?'

'The boat went down too suddenly for us to get hold of either.'

'The storm must have been a very severe one, then?' observed Waters.

'It was.'

'You were obviously near the coast. Couldn't you have run for shelter?'

'We didn't think the storm was going to be as bad as it turned out.'

'You didn't listen to any weather forecasts?'

'Summer storms in the Med often come out of the blue.'

'I didn't know they came quite that quickly.'

'It sounds like neither of you was very experienced?' said Turner.

'Certainly not experienced enough.'

'How d'you know your mate drowned?'

'I don't. But I checked before leaving Spain and his body hadn't been recovered. I went down to see Mrs Stevens to find out if she'd heard anything.'

'Had she?'

'No, she hadn't.'

'What's happened since then?'

'She's been on to the Spanish authorities, but they know nothing more.'

'You've been keeping in touch with her, then?'

'You know damn well I've seen her since.'

'Do we?'

'That dirty-minded detective must have told you we have.'

'Which one? There are so many dirty-minded detectives.' He paused for an answer he did not expect. 'The truth is, isn't it, that you see a lot of her?'

'No.'

'Especially before your wife died.'

'Goddamnit, why won't you listen to what I tell you?'

'Listening is easy; it's the believing which comes more difficult.'

Waters said: 'I reckon we've covered enough. Thanks for coming along for the chat.'

Weston said heatedly: 'I've told you the truth.'

'I'm sure you have.'

Across the table, Turner smiled sarcastically.

Having seen Weston off, Turner and Waters made their way across the front room to the lift. Inside, Turner pressed the button for the third floor. The doors slid shut.

'Have you ever messed around in boats?' Waters asked, as the lift started.

'Depends what kind of messing you mean?'

'Not the kind you're thinking about.'

'I was going to say, the back of a car's more comfortable.'

The lift slowed. 'If you had, you'd now be wondering just how stupid a man has to be if he sails into the teeth of a gale when he could turn and run for shelter.'

'What kind of an answer have you come up with?'

The lift stopped and the doors opened.

'Bloody stupid.' Waters stepped out. 'But Weston's not stupid and he's no gung-ho character, so there has to be something wrong with his story.'

They walked down the corridor. 'What are you going to do about it?' asked Turner as they came to a stop in front of the doorway into the CID general room.

'Think on it and then maybe have a word with the DI and see if he'll agree to forwarding a request to the Spanish police to see if they can find out anything about what went on down there.'

Mrs Ackroyd lived with her husband and younger son in the outskirts of Birmingham. She asked the PC into the sitting-room. 'You want me to look at some photographs?'

'That's right. If you'd just say if the man in 'em is one of the two you saw leaving the house in Trefoil Road.'

'You do understand that I wasn't taking any special notice of them? In fact, I couldn't really make out one of them at all.'

'I'll pass what you say on to London. Now, if you would just have a look.' He handed her four photographs.

She looked through them. 'He's certainly not the man I could see the more clearly. And I doubt he was the other one, either.'

Rentlow sat on the edge of his desk. 'You want me to forward a request through Interpol to ask the Spanish police to find out what they can about Weston's stay in Restina; in particular, whether he was there in the company of

Mrs Stevens? And what were the circumstances of the shipwreck?'

'Yes, sir,' replied Waters.

'To justify that sort of a request, I'll have to maintain that the potential evidence is vital to the case. Yet if Weston didn't kill his wife, it's totally irrelevant.'

'That's a big "If".'

'You can say that after Mrs Ackroyd's evidence?'

'It seems she wasn't all that certain about the second man. Secondly, Weston doesn't have had to have been one of the two to have set up the murder. Thirdly, there's something very wrong with his story about the shipwreck. Fourthly, almost all the other evidence names him murderer.'

'You're calling it evidence now? You're beginning to sound like Phil.'

'He has to be right occasionally.'

CHAPTER 19

Weston turned into the drive of Melton Cottage and parked by the side of the garage. He walked round to the front door, rang the bell. There was no response. He did not immediately return to his car, but stared out across the garden at the woods and watched a pigeon glide in and then, with an abrupt clap of wings, drop into an oak tree. He could have phoned to make certain she would be in, but he'd decided not to—if given the chance, she might well have refused to see him. It had been an unfortunate decision.

He began to walk back along the brick path to the garden gate, heard a car enter the drive. By taking one more pace forward, he was able to look past the corner of the house and was in time to see the tail of a red car disappear behind the outbuilding. He waited, warmed by the sun.

Her firm footsteps crunched on the gravel surface of the drive, the hinges of the gate squealed, and she came into sight. 'I thought I recognized the car. What do you want?' Her tone was bitter. She passed him, went up to the front door, then turned. 'Would you mind telling me and then going?'

'I've come to apologize.'

She could not conceal her surprise.

'I'm terribly sorry about last week. My only excuse is that I was so shaken by everything that I couldn't think straight and didn't really know what I was saying.'

She acknowledged that he might deliberately be provoking her sympathy in order to lessen her resentment, but had experienced sufficient grief in the past to be unable to stifle that sympathy. She unlocked the door. 'You'd better come on in.'

He followed her into the hall and through to the sitting-room. She sat by the side of the window, fingers joined and her hands in her lap; he remained standing just inside the doorway. 'Last week . . . You know what happened last week. This morning, I was asked to go along to the local police headquarters; it was more of an order than a request. Two detectives told me that the full post-mortem on my wife had been completed and that showed she did not die in an accident—she was assaulted by someone, managed to escape and in a complete panic ran, hit the banisters, and overbalanced. They call it constructive murder.'

'Oh my God!' she murmured.

'So now they're looking for the murderer and the way they questioned me made it very clear they think they've found him. But I've never used physical violence on any woman, least of all on my wife. I swear that that's the truth.'

'Why . . . why do they think it could have been you?'

'Because they're like Pavlov's dogs. By far the majority of murders are committed by someone in the family or a close friend, so initially they automatically suspect a family member.'

'But they have to find a reason, surely?'

'Nothing easier, when they're satisfied they're right. They twist the facts to suit their theory.'

'What theory?'

'That a relatively poor man married to a rich woman is only interested in her money; that if the marriage isn't one long honeymoon, he's planning to get rid of her because that's the only way in which he can hang on to the money; that if he's spoken to another woman more than once, she's his girlfriend . . . You were just too goddamn right. That ferrety detective who saw you did think we were lovers; so did the two detectives this morning. I told them I hardly knew you and they couldn't understand how I could be so soft as to expect them to believe that. The stupid bastards are convinced I killed Stephanie in order to inherit all her money and marry you.'

She unlocked her fingers, reached up and brushed a stray lock of hair away from her forehead.

He moved from the doorway, slumped down on the nearest chair. 'I've always thought the police in this country worked on hard facts. But they've decided I was guilty just because Stephanie's mother was vindictive enough to say I'd murdered her daughter.'

'That must be quite a strong reason.'

'Then you think they're in the right?'

'All I'm saying is, if a wife's mother accuses a son-in-law of murdering her daughter, the police are bound to suspect him. After all, there have to be pretty unusual circumstances for a mother to behave like that.'

'There were unusual circumstances, bloody unusual, but

they concerned Monica and her husband, not Stephanie and me. I tried to explain that to the police, but they wouldn't listen because what I told them didn't fit their theories. So how in God's name am I to convince them I didn't kill her; that not every husband lusts after his wife's money; that one can speak to a woman twice and not be bedding her? . . . I'm sorry. I came here to apologize and I've ended up by becoming hysterical.'

'That's hardly how I'd describe it.'

'The truth is, I'm . . .' He stopped.

She studied his face. 'Scared?'

'I know I'm innocent. Yet I see them becoming more and more certain I'm guilty.'

'You've no idea who the murderer could be?'

'The police say it can't have been a casual intruder who was surprised by her; but there's no one she knew who could do such a thing. And as for believing I could . . .'

'Since you didn't, no one will ever be able to prove that you did.'

'A month ago I'd have agreed. Innocence was the perfect shield. But I'm discovering that the shield's a bloody illusion.'

'I hope you're terribly wrong.'

'I know I'm terribly right.'

They were silent for a while, then she said: 'Would you like a drink?' It was nearly dusk. The light breeze had died away and the air had stilled so that noise travelled easily; as they stood outside the front door, they could hear a distant baler thudding rhythmically, a bulling cow, the crowing of a cockerel which seemed to have a confused sense of time, a barking dog, and an approaching car.

Weston stared at the Bramley in the bed in the lawn. 'Have I told you about Jason and that apple tree?'

'No.'

'He was very nostalgic about it and that surprised me because I'd have said he was the last person to indulge in nostalgia. It was probably a symbol for him.'

'A symbol of what?'

'Perhaps the promise that he could return here to a life of real values if ever he wanted to.'

She folded her arms across her chest as she stared at the tree; in the fading light, some of the lines in her face became lost and she looked young and more vulnerable. 'I wonder if he could ever really have settled down? There always seemed to be too much happening in his world for that. When I was a kid, I used to think him quite wonderful because he was so full of life; when I became an adult, I began to see that it was a destructive element of challenge which drove him on and would probably end up by destroying him . . . Perhaps one should be grateful he died before he discovered that in the end he had to be a loser. It's not a pleasant world for losers.'

Weren't all three of them losers? he thought bitterly. He said: 'I'd better start driving.'

They walked round to the Sierra. She faced him. 'I want you to understand that I'm very glad you came here this evening.'

'I just hope I haven't been too much of a Cassandra.'

'Didn't she foretell future woes that weren't believed rather than past ones which are? . . . It's helped me to talk things over; hasn't it done the same for you?'

'Yes, it has,' he answered, trying to sound sincere. Her sympathy was balm, but it couldn't alter facts. He opened the car door, but did not immediately climb in. 'If I drove down here again, would you come out and have a meal with me?'

She was as direct as ever. 'I'd like to.'

'I'll bring a signed pledge that there'll be no more groans and moans.'

'Unnecessary.'

He settled behind the wheel, lowered the window. 'Then it's au revoir.'

She bent down. 'Do you realize something? This is the first time we haven't parted in anger!'

The first two weeks in August brought hotter weather; temperatures rose until they were at record levels. Newspapers became filled with articles on skin cancer, drought, water restrictions, and greenhouse effect. Englishmen did like to take their pleasures morbidly.

Rentlow had finally given the temperature best and his coat now hung on the back of his chair; his braces were a fiery red. Waters, surprised by such a display of déshabillé, stared at the braces and tried to make out the pattern on them.

'Well?'

He jerked his mind back to more important matters. 'There's a report in from Spain re the Weston case.'

'Have they come up with anything useful?'

Waters put a sheet of paper down on the desk. 'I don't know who did the translation, but the meaning's mostly clear.'

Rentlow read the report. He looked up. 'Nothing changes. The hotel says he had a single room, but can't determine whether or not it stayed single. The police trace a witness who claims to remember seeing Weston in a night-club with two women but can't be certain whether or not one of them had red hair ... It's a case of lost opportunities.'

'Over the page is more definite.'

Rentlow turned the page. 'Good God!' he said, after a moment.

'It could explain a lot.'

'It could explain everything or it could leave us even

more confused than we are now ... The police claim he was engaged with Farley in drug-running. So did his wife discover what he'd been up to and he killed her to keep her mouth shut? Did he let slip that his wife was getting ready to loosen her tongue and the men at the head of the cartel decided they had to act. Or is this new information irrelevant to our case?'

Waters shrugged his shoulders.

'That's rather how I feel right now.'

'The Spanish police are going to ask for extradition.'

'I can read,' said Rentlow drily.

'How will you react?'

'With enthusiasm.'

'You're going to let them take him off our hands?' Waters was surprised. Even if that would remove an unpromising case from their statistics, Rentlow hated failure.

'I'm going to show a willingness to let them do so. A very different matter.'

'I'm afraid I'm not on your wavelength, sir.'

'Perhaps I should commend you for a lack of imagination.'

Waters couldn't understand why he was being mocked.

CHAPTER 20

The CID Escort slowed down. Waters, who was driving, said: 'It's that house.'

Rentlow stared through the side window. 'The very soul of pretentious respectability. Reminds me of my first raid, when I was a sprog; that house also looked as if it was occupied by an elderly banker without any taste but not a dirty thought in fifty years.'

'But it wasn't?' Waters edged into a parking space.

'The couple were running an abortion factory and making far more money than any respectable banker.'

They left the car and walked along the pavement to Francavilla. The gardener was weeding one of the beds in the front garden and he looked up, but merely nodded his head in reply to Rentlow's brisk good morning.

Mrs Amis opened the door. 'Yes?'

Rentlow introduced himself. 'We'd like a word with Mr Weston.'

She let them in and in silence led the way into the drawing-room. Before leaving, she stared round to make certain that nothing had been left lying about which might tempt a light-fingered policeman.

Rentlow went over to the nearest window and stared out at the back garden. 'One of the eccentric Dukes of Bedford instructed his staff to be as rude as possible to any visitor in the hopes that that would annoy him so much he'd leave. Perhaps Weston borrowed the idea?'

'I'd say it comes naturally to her. But underneath I'd guess she's not as spiky as she appears to be.'

'One day, Nick, your generosity of judgement will land you in trouble.'

It was seldom that the DI called Waters by his christian name. He wondered what had caused this touch of informality?

Weston entered the room. Rentlow introduced himself, then proceeded to take control of the meeting as if he were the host. 'We won't bother you any longer than we have to, but there is quite a lot to discuss so it'll be better if we sit.' He made himself comfortable. 'As you know, we've been making inquiries into the unfortunate death of your wife and these have shown that she was the victim of a constructive murder. Now, the law is both clear and unclear about such details. If the guilty person intended to kill the victim, though not necessarily in the way in which death eventually occurred, that is murder; if he did not intend actually to kill the victim, but was careless about the consequences of his actions and those actions would, in the judgement of any reasonable person, be likely to result in death, that is manslaughter. I'm sure you'll understand that where the law is unclear is in the grey area where the facts of the case don't obviously and clearly determine intention or the degree of carelessness. The practical consequences for the guilty man of the difference between murder and manslaughter are considerable; the one crime carries, both in theory and practice, a much higher penalty than the other—and I'm talking about moral consequences as much as legal. You'll understand why I'm telling you all this?'

'No,' replied Weston tightly.

'No? I will try to explain. It is often in the interests of the person guilty of having caused a death to admit to the facts if these indicate manslaughter rather than to continue to deny them, because by his admission he is indicating remorse and a willingness to suffer the punishment through which he will gain absolution. Judges when sentencing are always swayed by evident contrition. By contrast, however, if a man continues to deny everything, but the truth is exposed, the judge sees someone who knows no remorse and seeks no absolution. Judges tend to treat such men with great severity; being placed beyond temptation, they cannot understand many human frailties.'

'I had nothing to do with the death of my wife.'

'The facts suggest otherwise.'

'What the hell do any of you know about facts? You're only interested in automatic assumptions.'

'You aren't ready to tell us the truth?'

'I've told you the truth from the beginning.'

'You've nothing more to say to us now?'

'No.'

'I'm sorry. I was hoping you would have, for your sake.'

'Now you'd like me to believe that a false confession would be in my interests?'

'To understand that a true confession would be. Spain is to ask for your extradition. That would be denied if you pleaded guilty to manslaughter in this country.'

'Spain's doing what?'

'Asking for your extradition on the grounds that you have been engaged in drug-trafficking.'

Weston stared at Rentlow, for the moment unable to do anything but, ridiculously, wonder if he'd gone mad.

'They say that you loaded a tonne of cannabis resin off the coast of Morocco, intending to import it into Spain.'

'They're up the bloody pole.'

'When you sailed from Restina, you headed north in order to give the impression you were merely cruising up the Spanish coast; you altered course after dark and crossed to Menache; you returned on a reciprocal course and then turned south, in order to strengthen the deception that you'd been cruising. The plan was shattered by the storm.'

Waters, breaking a long silence on his part, said: 'One thing's puzzled me from the moment you told us about the trip—why didn't you run for the nearest shelter when it was obvious the storm was becoming fierce? Now it's obvious why. You didn't dare touch land before you reached Restina because it was there that you'd made arrangements for handling the cargo.'

'We didn't have an ounce of cannabis aboard.'

'The Spanish police say they have proof.'

'Then they're lying.'

'That's rather a wild accusation,' observed Rentlow calmly. 'Perhaps you should understand something. In the drug trade it's very much a case of dog eats dog. So a dealer will sell a quantity of drugs to a trafficker and then, after the latter has set sail, informs the authorities of the sale.

They, in turn, inform the police of the country of destination and the trafficker is arrested. Whereupon the dealer is given a reward for his information—usually a percentage of the value of the cargo. For the dealer, it's a case of eating his cake and having it.'

'No dealer could have informed on us because we didn't buy any drugs.'

'Did you sail to Morocco?'

'We cruised along the coast of Spain.'

Rentlow sighed. 'I can never understand why perfectly intelligent people insist on continuing to lie long after it has to be obvious that they are. Have you seen the inside of a Spanish jail?'

'Of course not.'

Rentlow smiled sardonically. 'Wealth, Mr Weston, doesn't always insulate one from the real world . . . Spain has a very ambitious programme for upgrading her jails, but unfortunately, as happens in every country, ambitions have become blunted by bureaucratic delay, inflationary pressures, and little brown envelopes. I'm told that so far only relatively few jails have been either rebuilt or modernized, so the majority remain as they were. I once had occasion to arrest a man who'd spent five years in a Spanish jail. He said that after that experience, the prospect of ten years in Dartmoor was a doddle. Degrading conditions degrade and human nature being what it is, a degraded prisoner often finds pleasure in dragging another down to his level; more pleasure if such person is a foreigner; the maximum possible pleasure if that foreigner is from a privileged background. I very much doubt that you can conceive the conditions of filth, casual brutality, and sexual harassment that can pertain in an old, overcrowded jail. I am certain that you could not endure them unscathed, both physically and mentally.'

'I'm innocent,' Weston said wildly.

'Then one can only hope that for your sake you manage to convince the Spanish authorities of that fact ... Of course, even if you eventually do, a remand in custody can be only a little short of a life sentence, not least because the motto of their legal service is, mañana never comes. Frankly, I'm surprised you're refusing to take the one step to avoid all that.'

'What step?'

'Telling us the truth about your wife's death. Obviously, if you're on a charge of manslaughter in this country, you will not be extradited to Spain on the charge of drug-trafficking.'

'I've told you all I know.'

'You've told us nothing.'

'Because I know nothing.'

'Unfortunate, from your point of view.'

'Why the hell won't you believe me?'

'Because you are lying.'

'It's the truth, goddamn it. Except for the trip in the boat, I've lied about nothing.'

'What about the trip?'

Weston could feel the cold sweat standing out on his forehead. Unlike Ulysses, he could not have himself tied to the mast as he approached Scylla and Charybdis. 'All right, we didn't cruise along the coast and we did cross to Morocco. But we picked up three men, not drugs. And when Jason said we had to run for port because of the weather, one of them pulled a gun amd made us sail on.'

'Were the three men Spaniards?'

'They certainly spoke Spanish amongst themselves and Jason said they were.'

'Then they were probably drug barons.'

'They weren't.'

'What makes you so certain when you can't even be positive about their nationalities?'

'Jason wouldn't have let them aboard if they had been.'

'Degrees of conscience? In my experience, conscience recognizes only one boundary; the probability of exposure. If not drug barons, terrorists?'

'They didn't look like terrorists.'

'Not even the one who pulled a gun on you? Not all terrorists resemble Che Guevara. How much were you being paid?'

'I refused to accept anything.'

'Back to the man of principles?'

'I crewed the *Cristina* only because I had to.'

'Shanghaied, no doubt?'

'I was blackmailed into it.'

'An interesting alternative. How were you blackmailed?'

'Jason laid on a party with a couple of women and . . .'

'And what? Don't hesitate in consideration of our feelings. We're reasonably broad-minded.'

'He had photos taken of me with one of the women and threatened to publish them if I didn't help.'

'With friends like yours, who needs enemies? . . . Well, all we can do now is observe routine. We'll inform the Spanish authorities that you deny having handled drugs and that you claim your cargo was three men, probably of Spanish nationality. I should warn you that either they'll disbelieve your denial or else they'll assume the three men were terrorists, in which case they'll no doubt be even keener for your extradition.'

'You've got to tell them I was forced into crewing.'

'I'll add a footnote to that effect, but I'd imagine the nature of the blackmail will lessen its effect. Being caught *in flagrante delicto* tends to cause amused contempt rather than sympathetic understanding.'

'I don't give a damn what it does, that's the way it happened.'

'Since it'll take time for our report to reach the Spanish

authorities and their modified request for extradition to
reach us, you'll be remaining at liberty for a while. It might
occur to you to leave the country and seek refuge somewhere where there's no extradition either to Spain or here,
so I'm going to ask you for your passport. You are at liberty
to refuse to give it to me. But if you do, I shall apply to the
courts for an order for confiscation and inevitably that will
cause publicity. You may prefer to avoid that?'

Weston wanted to shout that in a free country an innocent man couldn't be treated like a criminal, but retained
a sufficient sense of reality to understand that he could. He
left, went through to the library, returned with his passport.

Rentlow said to Waters: 'Write out a receipt.'

Waters had half a dozen blank receipt forms in the back
of his notebook and he filled in and signed one of these. He
handed it to Weston.

'Until we're in touch again,' said Rentlow, 'take time off
to remember that you can still reconsider.'

'Reconsider what?'

'That you may well avoid the exceedingly unpleasant
experience of a jail sentence in Spain if you decide to tell
us the truth about your wife's death.'

'I've told you it, over and over again.'

'A pity.'

They left. Waters settled behind the wheel of the Escort.
Rentlow clipped home his seat-belt. 'Goddamn it, you'd
have thought he'd have enough common sense to see where
his interests lay.'

Waters started the engine. 'Are the Spanish jails really
as bad as you suggested?'

'I've no idea . . . Well, what do you make of things?'

'A bit like Hampton Court Maze. It gets more confusing,
the further in you go.' He drew out from the pavement.

'Is he telling the truth about the trip to Morocco?'

'He made it sound that way. But if the cargo wasn't

drugs, how come the Spanish police say they've the proof that it was?'

'A good question. To which the obvious answer is, he was lying. But since the Spaniards are likely to regard the attempted importation of three probable terrorists as a far more serious crime than that of a tonne of cannabis resin, why go out of his way to risk the more serious accusation? Can you think of an explanation?'

'I can't, no.'

'There is just the one obvious possibility, isn't there? That he was telling the truth?'

'I thought you were convinced he was lying?'

'I'm convinced only that, as you said, things are becoming more and more confusing.'

CHAPTER 21

Kate was lying in a hammock she had rigged up between an ash and an oak which grew just inside the west-facing thorn hedge when she heard a car drive in. She swore. The sky was cloudless, the sun hot, the wind no more than a zephyr, and the gentle sway of the hammock reminded her so strongly of afternoons when she and Jason had sailed the upper reaches of the Dart that she had almost recaptured the simplicity of those days . . .

Weston came round the corner of the house and walked towards the front door and even at a distance she could discern his expression of worry. She sat up, not without a lurch which had her gripping the sides of the hammock. 'I'm over here.'

He saw her and came across the lawn.

She carefully slid out of the hammock. 'Something's happened, hasn't it?'

'The police came to the house this morning to tell me Spain's asking for my extradition.'

'My God—why?'

'They claim they've proof Jason and I loaded a tonne of cannabis resin off the coast at Menache and were intending to smuggle it into Spain.'

Her anger was immediate. 'Ridiculous!'

'I told the Detective-Inspector that Jason wouldn't ever have touched drugs. I had to admit we picked up three men.'

'You told them that?'

'It's the truth.'

'Haven't you learned that sometimes the truth's too dangerous to be told?'

'I . . . I wasn't thinking all that clearly.'

'Or at all.'

'They questioned me first about Stephanie's death. Then they told me that the only way I could avoid ending up rotting in a Spanish jail was to confess I'd been responsible for her death, even though I hadn't intended to kill her . . .'

She interrupted him. 'I'm sorry, but I don't understand. What can the request for extradition have to do with your wife's death?'

'They coupled the two together to try to make me admit I'd killed her.'

'Look, let's go inside and I'll make some coffee. Coffee has magical properties, one of which is the ability to calm and soothe.'

He followed her into the house and through to the kitchen. She half-filled a kettle and put this on the Aga. 'I warn you, coffee-making needs to be a ritual.'

'Complete with incantations?'

'Of course.' She turned to smile at him. 'There you are! Even the thought of drinking it is enough to start you relaxing.'

'That's you, not the coffee.'

She opened a cupboard and brought out a white porcelain jug and drip filter, a filter paper, an electric high-speed grinder, and a tin of coffee beans. She three parts filled the grinder with beans. 'Blue Mountain, supplied by a firm in London.' She worked the grinder for several seconds, then released the button. 'Do you like Bourbons?'

'They're one of my favourite biscuits.'

'And mine. And because they are, I've always been very careful never to discover how many calories each biscuit contains.'

'You've small cause to worry.'

'For that, you may have as many as you can eat.'

The kettle began to whistle. She lifted it off the Aga, poured a little boiling water into the jug, emptied the jug, set the filter on it, half filled the filter with coffee, carefully poured on some water. 'The cups and saucers are behind you.'

The cupboard, set back, was not large and its top was stepped because it had been built out under the staircase. He brought out cups, saucers, and plates, and put them down on one of the working surfaces.

'The Bourbons are in the end tin on the second shelf down of that cupboard.' She pointed. 'Shall we be informal and not put them on a plate? I'm sure food taste's better when it's eaten informally. That's why picnics are such fun . . .'

As she chatted inconsequentially, he acknowledged that she had skilfully eased much of the sense of panic which had gripped him before. No longer did he feel like a fly trapped in a web, helplessly waiting for the spider to approach; however illogical, he was now ready to believe there must be some way in which he could tear himself free.

They returned to the garden. She said that there were deckchairs in the outbuilding, but was he still young enough at heart to sit on the grass? He was. She poured out coffee and passed him a cup. He drank. 'Well, what's your verdict?'

'The finest I've ever tasted.'

'What a diplomatic taste! But I suppose you could hardly say anything else after my build-up. Jason used to say I . . . Damn! I was going to talk endless trivialities only.'

'So that the coffee had plenty of time to work its magical powers? They'd have to be truly magical to make me forget for long.'

She put her cup and saucer down on the grass, nibbled a biscuit. 'Tell me exactly what happened on that trip.' She drew up her legs, put her interlocked hands around her knees, and stared across the garden at the thorn hedge which, because of the level of her eyes, cut out any view of the woods.

He spoke quickly, but without the earlier panicky fear. She listened in silence, occasionally briefly turning her head to look quickly at him, as if certain that something lay behind his words and she was trying to discern what that was. When he came to an end, she refilled their cups, then said: 'You were very near the coast when the boat foundered?'

'I'd been steering to the north, but without plotting the actual course there was no way I could accurately judge how much I was closing the coast. Ironically, if we'd stayed afloat, we'd have run aground before long.'

'Once you were in the water, would you have survived if you hadn't managed to grab hold of support?'

'I'm a reasonable swimmer, but not a strong one. The probability would have to be that I wouldn't have made the shore.'

'Is that to say that a strong swimmer might well have done?'

'Yes. But I was in touch with the police until I returned

home and you've been on to them since and there's been
no report of any survivors.'

'Jason was a strong swimmer, but with a shattered
shoulder . . . If he'd survived, he'd have been in touch to
tell me.' She was silent for a while, her gaze unfocused. A
butterfly flew past, catching her attention. She sighed. 'I've
accepted it's no good going on hoping . . .' She reached out
and picked a daisy, began to pluck the petals. 'Did the two
middle-aged men look to be in good physical condition?'

'More like tired businessmen who've not walked further
than from the car to the office in years.'

'So it's unlikely either of them could have swum ashore?'

'Highly unlikely, especially as they were both so seasick
that drowning would have been a relief.'

'Which leaves the third man. He was younger?'

'Younger and tougher and altogether different. But if
you're wondering if he made the shore, forget it. The police
haven't reported any other survivors . . .'

'But there must have been one other.'

'Why?'

'Jason planned everything; when he wanted to, he could
make a statue seem loquacious. Look how he didn't even
tell you where you were going until you were at sea. The
three passengers were obviously intending to make an
illegal entry into Spain and so one has to assume that they
wouldn't have shot their mouths off beforehand, even if
Jason had told them the route he intended to take, which
as I've just said, he wouldn't have done. So how could the
Spanish police know you sailed along the coast until dark
and then went across to Menache, returning the same way,
unless someone who was aboard has told them?'

He was silent for a while, then he said: 'That never
occurred to me . . . But hang on. Assume the third passenger did survive. Why should he tell the authorities anything,
since he certainly wouldn't want them to know he'd come

from Morocco? And even if he had to admit he'd been aboard the *Cristina*, why would he claim we'd been carrying cannabis resin when that would inevitably implicate him in the drug-trafficking? And if the Spanish police learned he'd been aboard, they'd surely have named him in the extradition request to help prove the facts?'

'I know, put like that it doesn't add up. But can't you see that the only way of explaining how the police knew your movements is to assume that someone else who was aboard has survived?'

'Who then inexplicably and falsely implicated himself?'

She finished the biscuit and absent-mindedly reached for another. 'Gary, have you the slightest idea why your wife was killed?'

'None whatsoever ... Are you really asking if, just between you and me, I was responsible?'

'No. I believe you're a man who couldn't even consider doing anything so beastly.'

There could be no mistaking her sincerity. 'I'm sorry. It's just that I'm ...'

'Worried half out of your mind?'

'And scared stiff. I tell the truth, but no one believes me; I'm in a tunnel and can't turn back, but at the far end there's only disaster; I'm innocent, but everyone is convinced I'm guilty.' His earlier panic was back.

'Not everyone.'

'Then why ask if I know why Stephanie was killed?' In his panic, he forgot that only a moment ago, he had accepted her belief in his innocence.

'Because it's important. Right now, far more important than who was guilty. Why should anyone want to kill her?'

'I don't give a damn what the police say, it must have been a casual thief whom she surprised.'

'Suppose they're right, though?'

'Then that leaves just one possible suspect, me.'

'Which is the logic which makes the police so certain that you're lying and why they view the evidence from one angle. But you know you're telling the truth, so you can view it from another. If there was no casual thief, there has to have been a motive for her murder. You say there could have been none. But could there have been a motive for yours?'

'Was she killed instead, or because, of me?' He stared into the distance. 'The only thing in the past years that could possibly have brought about that sort of situation is what happened in Spain.'

'Where you were forced to take part in something illegal. Even though it ended in disaster, someone may be determined to make certain that there's no general knowledge of the failure. Who more likely to be that determined than another survivor?'

He spoke slowly. 'According to the police, Stephanie's assailant had been choking her, she managed to break free, and in her panic she ran so wildly that she went into the banisters at full speed and toppled over. Was he trying to force her to say where I was?'

'Did she know?'

'She went off to her mother's and I decided on the spur of the moment to come down here to see you. So she couldn't have told him where I was.' All too clearly, he could imagine her frantic terror.

She said softly: 'I read the other day that when things get too horrific, the mind provides an escape by blocking out reality.'

How did one block out the reality of being strangled? 'I must tell the police.'

'What will you tell them?'

'That the murderer is probably the youngest of the three men we picked up from Morocco.'

'They'd only consider the possibility if they will accept the probability that you're innocent of your wife's death.

They've made it clear that they won't. In any case, they're bound to counter the suggestion with the same questions you put forward just now.'

He stared into the distance. 'Then there's nothing I can do.' If he had expected sympathy, he was disappointed.

'Spoken like a wimp!'

He turned. Her expression was one of fierce determination. He said: 'When one's flat on the ground, one tends to feel rather like a wimp.'

'Only if one doesn't struggle. You're a struggler.'

'What makes you so certain?'

'Because I can always tell what a person is really like under the mask.'

'Were you able to tell what kind of a person your husband really was?'

She drew in her breath sharply. 'That . . . that's unfair. I knew he was weak and needed support; it was myself I didn't read.'

He bitterly regretted his words. 'I'm sorry, I should never have said that.'

'I've been saying things I shouldn't. Shall we call it quits?'

He nodded.

She cleared her throat. 'When you were here before, you said that some time you'd like to take me out to a meal. How about this evening?'

'The last meal of the condemned man?' But he asked with a touch of sardonic humour, not wimpish resignation.

They found that they had much in common. They both liked travel, orchestral music and operas, films without gratuitous violence, and nature documentaries on the television; they both disliked hypocrites, politicians (if these two were different categories), snobs, and unwillingly listening to a neighbour's hi-fi.

At a quarter past eight she suggested they drove to the pub in the next village which had only recently opened a restaurant so that the chef had not yet had time to become complacent. Her recommendation proved to be deserved. The menu was not elaborate, but the food was well cooked and presented, none of the vegetables had ever seen a deep freeze, and the management were satisfied with only a hundred per cent profit on the wine.

Weston emptied the bottle of Beaune into their glasses. 'This beats home cooking any day of the week. And before you take offence, I hasten to add that I'm referring to my home cooking.'

'Your dragon-daily believes in bangers and mash with sloshy cabbage?'

'Mrs Amis refuses to cook for me. It probably is a mercy in disguise. I have a feeling that rather than bangers, she's a boiled beef and dumplings enthusiast. I've loathed both even since my St Brede's days.'

She began to fidget with her wine glass, twisting the stem between thumb and forefinger. 'Did you enjoy your time there?'

'I'm not certain. Looking back, I remember mostly the highlights, seasoned with nostalgia. But I seem to recall telling my parents that I'd rather be in solitary confinement in prison.'

'How friendly were you with Jason?'

'There's no simple answer to that.' He drank. 'Like the others, I was slightly in awe of him because he deliberately lived life so dangerously. Awe sets up a reserve and danger tends to make one try to keep a safe distance. But we got on sufficiently well that from time to time I joined in with him ... and occasionally ended up in front of the head-master. I can't say my feelings were friendly at those times!'

'D'you know, I've never learned the truth about his expulsion. When it happened, I was considered too young to be told the details and in later years all Jason would do was roar with laughter and say that some experiences were worth their expense and some weren't. A girl was involved?'

'The headmaster's elder daughter. Jason was caught entertaining her in the headmaster's day study.'

'That really was asking for trouble! Did he choose both the girl and the location because that made the seduction so much more dangerously satisfying?'

'In one.'

'His report could have read, a sense of humour enclosed inside a fatal sense of judgement . . . He didn't suggest you kept him company with the younger daughter? Or was she that much too young?'

'He did and she wasn't, but luckily for once I had the courage to chicken out.'

'Then why didn't you do the same over the trip on the *Cristina*?'

'I didn't have the option.'

'Because he forced you into crewing. But if you hadn't met him since the day he was expelled, what on earth could he have had on you to make you take such a risk?'

'Initially, I had no idea I was taking any risk.'

'Are you going to explain?'

He didn't answer.

After a while, she said: 'Did Jason tell you anything about the background of the three men you picked up from Menache?'

'Not a damned thing.'

'So there's no way you can begin to identify them?'

'No.'

'Why were they going to Restina?'

'Your guess is as good as mine. Mine is that Jason had an arrangement with the harbourmaster and the local police and so if five men left the boat when only two had boarded, no questions would be asked.'

'It's . . .' She stopped.

'You were no doubt going to say, it's bloody hopeless.'

'Damn it, why the hell can I never learn to keep my big mouth shut? This was meant to be a fun meal . . . But all I was trying to do was to think up some way to help. Who was it said that he feared another's hatred, but was terrified by his help?' She reached across the table and put her hand on his. 'Something will break your way.'

He managed to nod.

The waitress, who also served behind the bar, came through and asked them what they wanted for sweet. They both chose chocolate mousse. He ordered a half bottle of white Bach. Drowning one's sorrows, it was called.

He turned into the drive of Melton Cottage and stopped in front of the garage. 'I owe you for taking me out of myself.'

'That's over-generous considering at one point I was doing my best to drop you back in! . . . Will you write me off as brazen if I suggest we do it again; soon?'

'Not brazen, just optimistic,'

'We're going to have the chance, don't make any mistake over that . . . Would you like some coffee before you drive back?'

'You're offering me a cup of magic?'

They walked round to the front door. In the hall she said: 'You go on through to the sitting-room and I'll make the coffee.'

'Not forgetting the incantations?'

He settled in one of the chairs, picked up a copy of *Country Life*, leafed through the house advertisements and then stopped to study the coloured photo and description of a hall house, set in seven acres. If only things had been different . . . His father had once said that 'If only' was responsible for nine-tenths of all duodenal ulcers.

She carried in a tray and set this down on an occasional

table. He watched her and noted how, as she bent, her cotton frock tightened across her right breast to outline it . . .

'A penny for them,' she said.

'I was thinking about duodenal ulcers.'

'Strange thoughts.' She smiled.

They talked about the countryside and how sad it was that so much of Kent was being ruined; they agreed that the ideal home was a period house with its own land all around and the nearest airport, motorway, railway, and hypermarket at least ten miles away.

The grandmother clock struck midnight as they were temporarily silent. 'Good God, I'd no idea it was that late! I must get moving.'

'You have an early appointment in the morning?'

'No.'

'Then why the panic?'

'Perhaps I'm worried that I've already overstayed my welcome.'

'A ridiculous panic.'

'Even so . . .'

'Even so?' she repeated mockingly.

'I'd better shift.' He was conscious that his voice had become strained.

'You demand the invitation in unambiguous words? . . . Stay.'

He stared at her, longing to accept without question, too honest with himself to do so. 'You don't have to just because you're sorry for me.'

'I could kick you where it really hurts! You think I'd invite you into my bed just because I felt sorry for you?'

CHAPTER 22

She left the bed, crossed to the window, and drew the curtains. The sunlight streamed in to set up highlights on her naked body. 'It's a lovely day.'

'So come back and celebrate.'

She returned to the bed, kissed him. 'It's too lovely to waste any of it. I'm going to have a shower and then get breakfast.' She smiled shyly. 'I've just realized I've no idea whether or not you like breakfast in bed?'

'I loathe it. I always spill crumbs which scratch.'

'I'm so glad. I always suspect that men who like breakfast in bed are suffering from the pasha syndrome.'

'So I was at grave risk of earning your severe disapproval?'

'Not really. I was certain you couldn't be one of them.'

'Then why bother to ask?'

'Do you always argue so much?'

'Only when I feel light-hearted from happiness.'

She kissed him again, went over to a bow-fronted chest-of-drawers and brought out of it clean underwear; as she moved around, he was convinced that she was revelling in displaying herself to him. She had proved herself to be a woman of passion; but a passion normally held under tight control because she was also a woman of emotion. During the night, she had told him that he was the first man she had known sexually since Ben had left her because she had to love to make love . . . He watched her leave to go through to the bathroom and he wondered why they could not have met years before? Perhaps if Jason had not been expelled . . . That damned 'If' . . .

She returned from the bathroom, dressed. 'Breakfast will

be on the table in fifteen minutes. Those who aren't down on time go hungry.'

'That's a sudden change of style! A moment ago I was being offered room service, now it's take it or leave it.'

'Hence the saying, seize your opportunities while you can or they may seize up.'

He sniffed. 'Something smells highly exotic.'

'A couple of months ago I was feeling so at the bottom of the world that I had to do something or cut my throat. I bought a very small bottle of Bejoule's *Le Rêve*.'

'And did it do the trick?'

'In a way. But in fact I never used it because when I got home I decided it had cost so much I'd have to keep it for a very, very special occasion.'

He laughed.

'That is a typical unthinking, unsympathetic male reaction,' she said scornfully.

He was enjoying a second cup of coffee when he said: 'What was the name of the scent you're using? Was it Boule?'

'Bejoule. Why d'you ask?'

'It seems to ring a bell, but I can't place why.'

'You've probably seen it mentioned in the glossy magazines. A couple of years back the firm was in financial trouble and was bought up by one of the big growers from Grasse and he's been spending a fortune on advertising. It's now so expensive that a woman has to feel guilty when she buys any.'

'Which, of course, is its real attraction . . . No, I'm sure I haven't seen it advertised. The name seems familiar for some other reason . . .'

'Turn your mind to more important things and decide where we're going today.'

*

They decided on a picnic. She had friends who lived in Sussex, but at the moment were abroad, and whose land ran down to a cove which, because the shoreline on either side was rocky, was seldom visited by other people.

They found they had the cove to themselves. They swam, assuring themselves it was delightfully fresh and not too cold for comfort, sunbathed, and as an apéritif drank the first bottle of white wine. They ate the ham, cheese, and scrambled egg with pickles, rolls she'd prepared at home, the éclairs they'd bought, and drank half the second bottle of wine. Then they sunbathed once more. She held his hand. 'If I could rub an old brass pot and summon up a genie, I'd order him to make here and now last for ever.'

'We'll start searching all the junk shops.'

'If only life could be so kind.'

They were unfortunate words because they brought back the idea of reality. The good times always came to an end; the bad times could last for ever.

'Stop it,' she said fiercely. 'You're not playing "I wish"; you're remembering, worrying, and seeing disasters by the score.'

He gently disengaged his hand, came to his feet, and slipped on his shoes to walk over the pebbles to the water's edge. ''Tis better to have loved and lost Than never to have loved at all.' Did memories of past happiness insulate or merely aggravate the present and future?

The theory of chaos was said to suggest that if a butterfly flapped its wings in Chile, a storm could sweep across England. An insignificant incident leading to massive destruction. Because he had been seated at that café in Restina when Farley had been passing, men had died and now he faced disaster. Step by step he mentally followed the route which had brought him to this point. The party at El Diablo, the voyage to Menache, the storm, the passenger too fanatical to appreciate the danger of what he demanded . . .

He returned to the travelling rug, sat. 'I've just remembered something.'

'What?' she asked sleepily, not bothering to open her eyes.

'Why the name of your scent seemed familiar. It's very like the name Bajols and that's where the three men on the *Cristina* were going.'

She sat up, hands around her knees. 'Have you any idea why they were so pressed to get there?'

'No, but obviously it was extremely important. If we'd run for safety, we'd probably have been able to set sail again within forty-eight hours. I wonder . . .'

'Spell it out.'

'It probably sounds crazy, but could there be some connection between their suicidal need to hurry and the false accusation of drug-trafficking that's supporting the request for my extradition?'

'Can you suggest what that could be?'

'Damned if I can. But as Holmes said, when you've eliminated the impossible, whatever remains, however improbable, must be the truth.'

'The idea's certainly improbable.'

'I know, but . . . One violent event can happen without any logical reason. But two, in pretty quick succession, involving the same person and without cause, is really stretching coincidence. And if that person then finds himself caught up in a false accusation which comes from the country in which the first act of violence happened . . . There would have to be a thread which runs through everything. Identify that and the logic of events would become apparent; understand the logic and one would have the answers.'

'Does all that get you anywhere?'

'It takes me to the possibility that if I could find out why the three men so desperately wanted to arrive at Bajols on time, couldn't wait even when their own safety was involved, then probably I could identify the thread, the logic, and the facts.'

'How can you hope to find out?'

'By going to Bajols and sniffing around.'

'That's crazy.'

'Why?'

'Because the odds are all against you finding out anything.'

'If I stay here, the certainty is that I'll find out nothing.'

'If the Spanish police learn you're in Spain, they'll arrest you.'

'In that case, I'll plead in mitigation of sentence that I've saved them all the hassle of extraditing me from England.'

'For God's sake, don't try to make light of things with feeble jokes.'

'Sorry.'

'Suppose you're right. And you find out something important. They murdered your wife, they murdered Jason. What do you think they'll do to you?'

'If I refuse to take the risk and stay here, then either I'm charged with the murder of Stephanie or I'm extradited on a charge of attempted drug-trafficking. I really haven't any choice, have I?'

'Not if you don't give a damn about me. And after all, why should you care about a one-night stand?'

'You don't understand . . .'

'No, I don't.' She stood. 'I want to go home.'

He broke a silence that had lasted for many minutes. 'God-damn it!' He braked the car to a halt, half on the verge of the country lane. 'I'm a complete fool. All my brave talk and I've completely forgotten that the police took my pass-port. So I can't search for threads; I'm grounded and all I can do is wait to discover whether I take up residence in an English or a Spanish jail.'

She raised her right arm, rested it on the back of his seat and ran her fingertips along his neck. 'I've only just found you, Gary, but that doesn't mean I can't love you through and through. But it does mean that the thought of your being killed turns me into a complete coward and that's why I was so bloody foul to you at the beach.'

'Forgotten.'

'But even as a coward, I know that you have to go to Bajols because that's your only chance of proving your innocence.'

'You're forgetting that I can't go anywhere without my passport.'

'Bloody marvel.'

'Come again?'

'Jason always called him that because he can forge anything.'

'Jason Farley?' said Pettifer, a tall, thin man, almost bald, with a prominent Adam's apple and a permanent look of disillusionment. He shook his head. He had never heard of Jason Farley.

Kate said briskly: 'You provided him with a forged VAT receipt for a yacht which he sailed to the Bahamas and sold to an American.'

He looked reproachfully at her. 'I know nothing about such things.'

'Jason admired you. He said you were very, very expensive, but worth every penny.'

The sound of money spurred his memory. 'You say that Jason Farley is your brother?'

'Yes.'

'He's never mentioned a sister.'

'Too ashamed of a respectable sibling.'

He cleared his throat. 'Can you prove you are his sister?'

'If I weren't, how would I know all about that VAT receipt?'

He had thick lips and he flipped his right forefinger backwards and forwards across the lower one. He looked at her, at Weston, and then at nothing in particular. 'I know nothing about false passports. But I have heard that it's still possible to obtain one with a false birth certificate. Of course, I've no idea how one goes about obtaining one of those . . .'

She interrupted him. 'We want it this time tomorrow.'

'Quite impossible.'

'How much?' asked Weston.

He stopped fiddling with his lip. 'If—and this is pure supposition, you must understand—I heard of one, it would certainly cost a great deal of money.'

Weston brought an envelope out of his pocket. 'There are two photos here, in case the first one gets messed up.'

'A passport would certainly cost three thousand pounds at the very least.'

Weston prepared to bargain.

CHAPTER 23

Bajols, seventy kilometres inland, had not been directly affected by the tourist trade which had so ravaged the coastline. Externally, the majority of houses remained unreformed and only a few new ones had recently been built. The town's primary concern was agriculture. It lay in a broad valley whose soil was unusually fertile and beneath which lay a virtually limitless supply of water. Even the lower slopes of the surrounding mountains grew rich grass and Bajols' lamb was recognized as far afield as Madrid as the best one could buy. Indirectly, however, the inhabitants were affected by tourism but, unusually, only to their benefit. Because of the tens of thousands of tourists on the coast, all produce could readily be sold at prices which made the old men shake their heads in disbelief. Those houses with bleak exteriors were more often that not luxuriously appointed inside.

Having nothing to offer the casual visitor, very few ever came. In consequence, the one small hotel was spotlessly clean, but lacked even primitive air-conditioning, the only hostal was even more spartan, restaurants served only local dishes, and the many bars still set a free dish of olives in front of every customer and then charged so little for the drinks that their counterparts on the coast would have been outraged.

Weston left the Hotel Victoria and stepped out into the fierce sunshine; within half a dozen paces he was sweating. At the end of the narrow road, overhung by balconies with elaborate wrought-ironwork, was the square and to the south side of this was a bar with half a dozen tables set outside under the cover of a tattered and faded sun blind. He sat at one that was in complete shade. A waiter, dressed in black trousers and white shirt, both of which had seen better days, asked him what he wanted. He ordered a gin and tonic and the waiter, lacking the xenophobic contempt for linguistic incompetence of a Frenchman, managed to understand him.

The drink and a small earthenware dish of olives were brought to the table. He drank, wiped the sweat from his forehead, stared across the square at a mule cart which slowly squeaked its way round to a side street, and wondered at the yawning gap between expectation and performance. In England, he'd optimistically assured himself he'd find the means of uncovering the truth and proving his innocence; here, after thirty-six hours, having tramped the town from end to end, he'd found out nothing which could conceivably do either. His trip had become a futile attempt to escape the inescapable.

He finished the drink, looked around for the waiter, stood and went over to the doorway. A handful of men, mostly elderly, were watching the television; the waiter, half asleep, was leaning against the bar. One of the viewers saw Weston and called out and the waiter started, stood upright. Weston raised his hand to his mouth to indicate another drink.

He returned to his seat and ate two more of the olives, even more bitter and peppery than the one he had tried in Casa Pep. When the drink came, he proffered a handful of coins. The waiter took a one hundred and a fifty peseta piece. He added another fifty and the waiter looked even more surprised than gratified.

He drank slowly. What in the hell did he do next? Where did one look for something which one couldn't identify, in a town which hibernated in the heat and which one had already explored? Logically, one gave up and admitted failure; caught the train back to Seville and from there flew home where one waited to be arrested either for one crime or for the other . . . Yet he still couldn't bring himself to accept the logic . . .

Doing nothing merely confirmed that he'd nothing to do. Action, any action, was preferable. He finished the drink, stood. The church was on the far side of the square and he hadn't yet visited it, so here was an objective. It was a bleak, architecturally very simple building, its sheer fifteen-metre walls of sandstone blocks unpierced by windows. But as with the houses, its exterior was a poor guide to its interior. Inside there was graceful form, beauty, and colour; thin columns of veined marble, stone figures carved with considerable skill, a wealth of gold leaf, a dome painted with a surprisingly robust allegorical scene, carved pews, and a magnificent reredos.

He was studying the reredos when he heard footsteps. A priest, short, tubby, with a round face that spoke of an unquestioning faith filled with good humour, came up the nave to stand by his side. The priest spoke in rapid Spanish, slurring his words as was the local custom.

'I'm sorry,' Weston said, 'I don't speak Spanish.'

'You is English? You is here to see that?' He pointed beyond the altar at the reredos.

It would have been churlish not to have agreed. 'I was told it was so beautiful I mustn't miss it.'

'Then you come.'

Weston followed the priest past the altar. The priest spoke with the excitement of someone eager to impart the reason for his enthusiasm. A hundred years ago, Bajols had been almost as well known for its woodcarving as its agriculture; traditionally, certain families had carved religious figures and these had been famous throughout the province; beyond the province, even, because a fiat had come from Seville to commission the leading carver—Bartolomé Vicens—to carve a Madonna and Child which would adorn the side chapel in which the Count of Huelva was entombed. The carving had taken months, some said years. It had been a labour of love. Others had tried to help, but Vicens had insisted on doing all the work himself—even such preliminary steps as would normally have been left to an apprentice. And since the carving had been hung in the chapel, miracles had been attributed to it and every year a mass was said for the soul of the man whose faith had wrought such beauty.

All the time he had been speaking, the priest had been running his fingertips over the wood; now, he dropped his hand away and his expression saddened. There had been woodcarvers in Bajols right up until the Civil War—though none as great as Bartolomé Vicens—but during that dreadful time the young had been called away and only the old

had remained. True, they had continued to work but without heart—how could they retain heart in such times? After
the war, only a few of the young had returned and they had
not wished to resume working in a job which called for faith
as well as skill—sadly, their faith had not survived—and
whose rewards were more to be measured in spiritual rather
than financial terms. So now there was no man in Bajols
who carved wood to the glory of God.

Weston thanked the priest and asked if he could make a
contribution to the church funds. He was shown a small
collection box and put a thousand-peseta note into this.
Clearly, it was regarded as a generous gift. The priest said
that it had been a pleasure to show the English señor the
treasure of the church; it would be a more selfish pleasure
to offer some simple hospitality and the door of his home,
No. 15, Calle General Pena, was always open . . .

Weston returned to the square and wondered how much
longer he was going to be fool enough to continue to search
for something that didn't exist.

Once it was dark, the heat abated slightly and some degree
of obvious life returned to the town. In the square, an ice-
cream stall opened up and a man with an ancient barrow
sold sweets in small packages to the children; women moved
chairs out into the streets and sat and gossiped; men filled
the bars and talked, argued, played cards and dominoes;
cars, a large number of them new, drove through the narrow, twisting streets, ignoring all road signs yet somehow
avoiding crashes . . .

Weston, once more without any objective, walked to the
end of the road to find himself on the edge of the village.
Ahead was a road and beyond that a football pitch, sharply
defined by arc lamps, from which came the sound of pop
music, played so loudly that it seemed to echo off the surrounding mountains. Watching a game would while away

more time, even if the game were between unidentified teams. The ticket office was a hole in the surrounding wall and a scrawled notice said that the entry fee was 200 pesetas. He paid, waited for the ticket and then realized none was being offered, went through the gateway.

The pitch was sand and the grandstand, half-full, consisted of three rows of concrete seats. He sat at the end of the middle one. The players were enthusiastic but lacking in basic skills and the ball went from end to end of the pitch, frequently as a consequence of mis-kicking. After fifteen minutes a goal was scored by the team with blue shirts and the roar of satisfaction suggested this was the home side. Soon afterwards the whistle blew for half-time.

Spectators stood, moved around, and shouted boisterously even when within easy earshot, children raced up and down the stand, and two men with trays on which were chilled bottles of beer, popcorn, cigarettes, and sweets, each extolling his wares at the expense of his rival, slowly went round the ground.

He was looking towards the entrance gateway when two municipal policemen in light blue shirts and dark blue trousers, radios strapped to one side of their belts, holstered guns to the other, strolled through. One of them shook hands with a spectator and began talking to him, the other, peaked cap tilted back on his head, hands on hips, stared around himself with the arrogant challenge of a bully in authority. With a sense of shock, Weston recognized the man who had shot Farley.

The policeman's gaze passed him, then abruptly returned. Even at that distance and in the uneven light from the arc lamps, it was possible to see his expression change from disbelief to vicious determination. He shouted to his companion, began to run, unbuttoning his holster as he did so.

There could be no escape the way Weston had entered

the ground since that was the only entrance/exit. But the third and highest row of seats was within a metre of the top of the wall. He pushed his way between a group of men who were chatting to reach the top row, scrambled up on to the wall, jumped down. As he landed with jarring force, there were shouts from inside.

He raced across the road and up the first street to reach the square, where he came to a panting halt. The two policemen would have sounded the alarm over their radios; while there were probably few other policemen on duty to join in the hunt, the fact that among the locals he stood out like a sore thumb made him immediately identifiable. So if he stayed on the streets he would soon be cornered; if he returned to the hotel he would be going to the first place his pursuers would search; if he left the village and struck out across the countryside, he would be in totally unknown territory and even if he survived the night, he must be picked up in daylight . . . He remembered Kate's fear of what would happen to him if he were recognized and how he'd so light-heartedly dismissed such a possibility.

He could clearly hear the noise of pursuit, which must mean that the van of his pursuers had entered the road to the square. Instinct demanded he run, but a man who ran attracted more attention than one who walked. He walked. He reached the road that ran up the side of the church and suddenly remembered the priest. If any man would accept his claim of innocence, surely the priest would? Yet even if he did, would that call forth an offer of practical help? But with no one else to turn to . . .

How to find Calle General Pena? Ask and it would take time for him to make the question understood, even more time for him to understand the answer, and he would have pinpointed his destination. Surely the priest would live near the church? But previous wanderings had shown that this was an area which was a warren of narrow, short roads.

He continued, to reach a T-junction. Turn right or left? The road to the right appeared to be lined with shops, while that to the left contained only houses on the opposite side from the church. He turned left. Fifteen paces on, he could see that the road ended at another T-junction immediately beyond the far corner of the church. Convinced he'd made the wrong choice, certain from the noise that his nearest pursuers must be almost on him, he whirled round and prepared to run—now less dangerous than walking. As he did so, he noticed that in the wall to his right were a doorway and windows and he realized that this was the priest's house, built on to the northern end of the church.

There was a shout, so loud that he was certain the man must be within feet of the T-junction. He grabbed the rusty door handle, turned and pushed. The door opened. He stepped inside, shut the door behind him.

He was in a small room, probably both entrance hall and reception room, lightly furnished with a couple of leather-backed chairs, a religious painting, a wooden chest with a vase of cut flowers, a threadbare carpet, and a table on which was a telephone that began to ring. The priest, now in open shirt and shorts, came through the nearer doorway and, seemingly not in the slightest surprised to see him, went over to the telephone. He lifted the receiver, listened, spoke rapidly to the accompaniment of many gesticulations of his free hand, then replaced the receiver. He smiled broadly. 'Is good to meet another time.'

'I'm in trouble. The police are searching for me.'

The priest's round, plump face expressed surprise. From outside, came the sounds of excited shouting. Then a car with a faulty exhaust went past to drown out all other noise and when it was gone the shouting was no longer audible.

'I swear I've done nothing wrong. But if the police catch me, I won't be able to prove that and they may kill me to make certain I never can.'

The priest's appearance suggested a simple man of simple faith; he was so, but, as had any middle-aged priest with humility, he'd come sympathetically to understand a little about human nature and usually to be able to distinguish truth from lies. After several seconds, he said: 'Come, please.'

They went into a room, larger than the first, which was far less impersonally tidy. A newspaper was spread out over one chair, a Siamese cat lay curled up in the second, a cigarette lay smoking in an ashtray, and Beethoven's Ninth was playing on a midi hi-fi. The priest switched off the record, shooed the cat from the chair, pointed. 'Please, sit yourself.' He carefully folded up the newspaper on the second chair, sat, stubbed out the cigarette. He picked up a pack and offered it.

'No, thanks.'

'Is small indulgence,' he said shyly. He waited a moment, then said: 'Please, you say what is trouble.'

Weston, speaking as simply as he could, briefly related what had happened. When he finished speaking, the priest, his head tilted slightly to one side, stared at him for several seconds and then, still without a word, stood, left the room. Weston stared at the closed door. Had the other decided that in the circumstances his duty had to be to report the matter to the police? After all, this was hardly a spiritual problem . . .

The priest returned, carrying a tray on which were a bottle and two glasses. 'Again a small indulgence.' He poured out two sherries, passed one schooner to Weston. 'What is name of policeman on boat?'

'I don't know. I never heard it.'

'How he look?'

He described the policeman he had recognized at the football field.

'He speak English well on boat?'

'He seemed to understand everything and was reasonably fluent, even if he got a word wrong now and then.'

'Perhaps is Victoriano Herrero.' He stood and began to pace the floor between the chair and the window; every third pace, he rose up on his toes as if about to hop. 'Is a man who . . .' He came to a sudden stop. 'When this happen at sea?'

Weston thought back. 'It was the night of the fourth that we picked them up; we sank in the early morning of the fifth.'

The priest had come to a stop. Now, he smacked his right clenched fist into the palm of his left hand. 'Agosto Seis!'

'What does that mean?'

'It is wicked men who . . . No, I shall not say such.' He sat, heavily, as if to punish his flesh for his lack of compassion. The cat, which had been lurking behind the chair, came round and jumped up on to his lap. He stroked it as he spoke excitedly, disjointedly, frequently reproaching himself for his judgements, yet never withdrawing them.

Throughout the troubled times of the first two decades of the present century, the loyalties of the inhabitants of Bajols and the surrounding countryside had not become polarized as had happened in so much of the rest of the country; perhaps the mountains had insulated them from inflamed passions.

But around nineteen-thirty things had changed. Some said that agitators had come all the way from Malaga where the Left had been very active—the priest did not know; he had not been born until the year war had broken out. There had been many incidents. The priest—in those days, there had been only the one in Bajols—had had his house burned down, a cabo in the guardia civil had shot and killed one of the agitators; men who had been friends from childhood became enemies. Bajols had turned into a town of hatreds . . .

Alfonso Bauzer, the younger son of the largest landowner in the valley, had been a colonel in the army. His father had been one of the fairest and most liberally minded of landowners, but Alfonso had been different. A man for whom charity, understanding, and mercy, were words of weakness . . .

'Is much wrong to speak so,' said the priest, even more angry than before at expressing a judgement that was not his to make. He finished his sherry, then proceeded to expand that judgement. Alfonso Bauzer had believed that most men were born to obey and only a few to order; that wealth was the right of the few, as poverty was the proper burden of the many.

In order to exterminate all dissent, he had taken command of Bajols and successfully called upon the guardia civil to support him. When news reached the town of the uprising in Morocco, he had demanded public rejoicing. When he had learned that Franco was flying from Morocco to Seville, he had rushed to Seville to arrive on the same day—the sixth of August—in order to pledge the loyalty of the valley.

In Bajols the guardia had carried out his orders with enthusiasm. Men and women were arrested; when the small jail was full, the bullring—now the football field—had been used to hold the captives. For weeks, every night a lorry had driven up to the bullring and taken aboard many prisoners and then made for the mountains; when it returned, it had been empty. Those who were not arrested were 'persuaded' to work for the cause and they had laboured in the fields from dawn to dusk and counted themselves lucky if paid . . .

Colonel Bauzer had left Bajols to fight for the Nationalists; General Bauzer had returned. The war had taught him nothing. The sight of endless suffering had merely hardened his mind and narrowed his vision . . .

The priest paused as if to admonish himself yet again, but then he continued without doing so; he found it easy to forgive those who had little, difficult to forgive those who had much.

The General had ruled the valley as if it had been his private fiefdom. His word was the law. When the statue of Franco had been erected in the square, he had let it be known that it would be suitable for a statue of himself—slightly smaller, but only slightly—to appear somewhere else. Soon, there was not only an Avenida Generalísimo Franco, there was also an Avenida Alfonso Bauzer. (Even one avenida in Bajols would have been an absurdity; there wasn't a street much wider than a mule cart.) And a Calle Agosto Seis to mark the day on which the Caudillo had met Bauzer in Seville. At one time, so it was said, men had walked to Calle Agosto Seis in order to urinate against the walls . . .

Alfonso Bauzer had died and then, two months later, so had Franco. Following the latter's death, it had been as if the country had suddenly been allowed to breathe. A king had come to the throne and brought democracy. Democracy had brought a socialist government . . . This had frightened those whose wealth was great, who had held power under the old regime, for whom the doctrine of equality was anathema. Several such men had come together in Bajols and formed an association known as Agosto Seis to commemorate the day on which their hero and the Caudillo had joined together to fight the Left. Initially, it had been a local party of dissidence; soon, however, its tentacles had reached as far as Madrid. To it had flocked men who sought what they thought they had lost, or what they could not hope to gain in the normal course of events. And when the government had decided that at long last there should be a redistribution of those vast tracts of land in Andalucia which made a handful of men millionaires but denied tens of thousands anything but a life of subsistence, those in Agosto Seis had talked about revolution . . .

Bajols, locked within a valley, had become the unlikely centre of a conspiracy to overthrow the newly acquired democracy. And since men who sought power usually hid their ambition under a cloak of hypocrisy that would attract the gullible, they had presented their aims as a desire to gain a return of family values—divorce was to be abolished, the pill to be forbidden, pornography to be destroyed—which so many wanted.

A conspiracy had to have a leader, even if only a figure-head. Jaime Bauzer. A very different man from his father, the General, but vain enough and weak enough to accept the position. Everyone but he accepted the fact that when Agosto Seis gained power, he would be deposed to be replaced by a man of steel . . .

The priest stood. 'Please, you stay.'

It was a quarter of an hour before he returned and, with apologies for having taken so long, handed Weston a cutting from a newspaper. This contained two photographs, one of a group of men, one of a man on his own. Weston identified the man on his own as one of the two who had stayed in the saloon of *Cristina II* throughout their return voyage.

'Is Jaime Bauzer. He drown on holiday in Marbella; friend also drown.'

CHAPTER 24

Weston crossed to the window and looked through a chink between curtain and frame. The priest had proved himself to have a developed cunning. He would park his car by the front door—no one would take any notice of it because he was often called out during the night—and as soon as the road was clear of traffic and pedestrians, Weston could climb into the back and hunker down. They would drive to Seville where Weston could catch the first plane to England. When he'd demurred at causing the priest so arduous a journey in the middle of the night, the other had replied simply that Herrero, sargento-in-charge of the municipal police, was a clever, hard, ambitious man, almost certainly highly connected in Agosto Seis, who'd go to any lengths to prevent the truth about Jaime Bauzer's death becoming known. He would have alerted the whole of the province to search for the Englishman who was travelling on a false passport—as the registration in the hotel would have shown—and since so many of the members of the Policia Armada y de Trafico, Municipal police, State police corps, and Guardia Civil, were members of Agosto Seis, the search would be as thorough as very determined men could make it . . .

Weston heard a car approach, then saw a Renault 19, but this carried on past. He watched it disappear from sight and wondered if the priest were right to be quite so confident that his comings and goings would be unremarked. In normal time, probably. But if Herrero was desperate to catch his quarry, wouldn't any movement, if in the slightest degree unusual, attract his attention?

The priest had briefly tried to explain why it was so important for the members of Agosto Seis to conceal the truth about Bauzer's death. Spaniards honoured symbols, often more than they did the reality behind them. To the members of Agosto Seis, General Bauzer had been not only the founder, but also their spiritual guide; August the sixth had been the day on which Franco, flying from Morocco, had had the good fortune to meet Bauzer in Seville—a meeting which had ensured the defeat of the Left. So what contemporary symbol could be more powerful than one which combined a Bauzer, Morocco, Seville, Bajols, and

August the sixth? Jaime Bauzer had travelled to Morocco in order to be clandestinely brought back to Spain in a boat skippered by an Englishman (Franco had travelled in an aeroplane clandestinely piloted by an Englishman); on landing, he would have travelled to Bajols and then to Seville, to arrive on August the sixth. There, he would have called on his supporters to rise up and strike the government who had betrayed Spain by opening their beloved country to the evils of socialism, foreign domination, the permissive society . . .

Nothing could deflate a cause and expose its absurdity more completely than laughter. What more humorous than a middle-aged, tubby, soft-living man setting out to mimic the Caudillo and the General and suffering an inglorious, seasick, helpless death by drowning even before he'd set one foot on the shores of Spain?

Yet all could still be saved if only it were generally accepted that Jaime Bauzer had died an accidental death, totally unconnected with the cause. Then, with no farcical memories fatally to mock, another man could step forward and, on a future August the sixth, proclaim the crusade in Seville. But for that course to succeed, there must be no foreign witness to the truth of Bauzer's death . . .

He heard another car approach and this one slowed, stopped. Even in the subdued street lighting, the green Seat Ritmo looked as if it had recently escaped from a breaker's yard. How on earth was that going to cross the mountains to Seville? On four bald tyres and a prayer?

He caught the tube at Heathrow and after one change arrived at Randall Common station. A taxi was waiting outside and he gave his address. The driver muttered bad-temperedly at the short fare.

He walked into the house, called out: 'Mrs Amis.'

She entered the hall from the service passage, handbag

in one hand and plastic mac in the other. 'It's you, is it? I'm off home, seeing it's time.' She challenged him to point out that she was leaving ten minutes early. 'I didn't know you was going to be away.'

'I didn't know myself until the very last minute. Have there been any alarms and excursions?'

'It's been quiet enough,' she answered reluctantly.

'Any messages?'

'I've wrote 'em all down.'

'What about visitors?'

'Only them two detectives.'

'What did they want?'

'You. I said I didn't know where you was. That made 'em a bit annoyed, but as I told 'em, it wasn't nothing to do with me. I'll be on my way, then.' She turned and began to walk towards the passage, then stopped. 'There was one phone call earlier today, but I didn't bother to write nothing, seeing there wasn't any message.'

'Who was it?'

'Wouldn't know, would I? He went on about it being so important to talk to you, but like I kept telling him, I couldn't say where you was, unless you was down in Kent.'

She went through the doorway.

'Mrs Amis,' he called out. When there was no immediate response, he hurriedly followed her. As he entered the passage, she was at the outside door. 'Hang on a sec.'

Reluctantly she let go of the door handle.

'Did you ask this man for his name?'

''Course I did. But he didn't answer and anyways, him being a foreigner, I wouldn't have understood.'

Fear stabbed his mind. 'How d'you know he was a foreigner?'

'Couldn't speak English proper. And what's more, he didn't thank me when I gave him the telephone number.'

'What telephone number?'

'Mrs Stevens's. Thought you might just be there.' She smiled slyly.

'You bloody fool!' he shouted.

She was shocked; not by the language, but by the certainty that for him to have spoken like that, she must unwittingly have done something very stupid. She began a mumbling apology, but he turned and raced back into the hall. She heard him lift the telephone receiver and dial, left, eager to escape any knowledge of the consequences of whatever it was she had done.

There was no reply. Kate was probably out, shopping or visiting; but she might be lying huddled on the floor, as Stephanie had lain, dead because she had not been able to say where he was. About to dial 999, he realized that on this occasion it would be much quicker to contact the divisional HQ. He found the number in the directory, dialled it and asked for Detective-Constable Turner or Detective-Sergeant Waters. He was connected to Waters.

'We were wondering where you were, Mr Weston . . .'

'Mrs Stevens may be in terrible trouble. You've got to get someone to her house to find out.'

'What exactly . . .'

'Never mind the bloody "whats".'

'I can't go asking favours of another force unless there's good reason. And just because you think Mrs Stevens might be in some sort of trouble . . .'

'Goddamnit, someone's looking for me and he may get hold of her and force her to say where I am. And she doesn't know, any more than Stephanie knew.'

'Have you thought of ringing her and warning her?'

'Of course I bloody well have. There's no answer.'

'Who do you think may be threatening her?'

'A Spaniard, Victoriano Herrero; he's a sergeant in the municipal police at Bajols.'

'You really think a Spanish policeman might come to England to try to find you . . .'

'To kill me. Christ, man, he spent all last night trying to do just that. The only way I managed to escape was because a priest helped me.'

'You have been to Spain?'

'How the hell could I have been in Bajols if not?'

'But you had no passport.'

If he were to persuade the Detective-Sergeant to act, then he was going to have to admit the truth—only a desperate man would make such an admission. 'I bought a false passport for two thousand pounds. For God's sake, get someone to drive to her place to see she's all right.' He replaced the receiver.

He went out, locked the front door, and as he withdrew the key, heard the phone ringing. The Detective-Sergeant, wanting to ask more questions? The Sierra was down in Kent, but the Mercedes was in the garage. It hadn't been on the road since the day Stephanie died, but the engine started first time. He backed down the drive, turned into the road, not bothering to stop to shut the garage doors; seconds could mean the difference between life and death.

He was not normally a fast driver, but now it was as if the hounds of hell were behind and closing; he took risks which at any other time would have left him sweating and shaken. One hour and twenty minutes after leaving Francavilla, he drove into Melton Cottage.

He was half out of the car when he heard the sounds of running feet and then Kate came in sight, grabbed him into her arms, demanded to know why a patrol car had called and two PCs had asked if she was in any trouble, and was he all right, really sure he was all right?

A patrol car turned into the drive at 4.15 and a uniform sergeant and PC walked round to the front door. Kate let them into the house and introduced them to Weston.

'Seems like everything's under control, then?' said the sergeant.

'It is, thank God,' replied Weston, 'but it very easily could not have been.'

'In our job, Mr Weston, there's always something nasty that could happen, but usually doesn't.' He looked a hard man, careless of others' emotions, but his quick smile suggested that his looks were deceptive. 'So you'll be around from now on, will you?'

'I very definitely will.'

'Then I don't suppose we need worry any more.'

'You won't be keeping a watch on here any longer?'

'It's like this. With so much territory to cover, a special watch on somewhere cuts out one being able to do our full job everywhere. So with you around, Mrs Stevens should be all right and we can keep moving. But if anything happens, just call for help and a patrol car will be with you before you've time to put the receiver down.'

It was obvious that he had to accept their assurances. He offered them a drink, which was refused, thanked them for all they'd done, and saw them out. As they went round the corner of the house, he wondered if his fears had been ridiculous? Perhaps he should have remembered that Mrs Amis was a walking catalogue of illogical dislikes and the caller might well not have been a foreigner, but merely someone speaking with a heavy regional accent.

Her bedroom, the largest of the three, was at the eastern end of the house and it had two sash windows and one dormer; the last, which faced the woods, an addition made by the previous owner. The ceiling was beamed and a built-in cupboard had been fashioned out of the space between the outside wall and the thick central chimney which rose up from the sitting-room and provided support for the roof.

She had furnished the room warmly, but without frills. She walked over from the doorway and sat on the end of the bed and stared up at him. Then she held out her hand and he took it; she pulled him down to her side, snuggled against him. 'I kept thinking of you. I tried to tell myself you were perfectly all right, but I couldn't stop imagining the most awful things. It got so bad that I took a pill to try to get some sleep, but that just gave me even worse nightmares. I read once that one doesn't dream when one has taken a sleeping pill; how bloody ignorant some writers are!

'I managed to sleep a little last night—without a pill. When I was awake I played a game which I used to when I was a kid. If something happened, everything would be all right; if I heard the cuckoo before ten, you'd be safe and sound. I'd heard it every morning for the past week, but this morning the bloody bird never made a cheep. Then I saw a police car drive in and I froze solid inside because I knew they'd come to tell me you'd been killed . . .

'They said they didn't know why, but they were here to make certain I was all right. I wanted to kiss them because I knew it meant you were alive and safe . . . Oh God, my darling, I've been through the wringer.' She saw he was about to speak. 'But you had to go and I had to stay. Women's lib hasn't altered that.' She hugged him harder. 'Now it's time to relax.'

'Sleep for twelve hours with nothing but dreams of verdant landscapes?'

'How little you know about women. Undress me.' She released him, stood.

She was wearing a cotton frock with a bright, floral design which unbuttoned down the front almost to waist level. He undid the buttons, reached down to take hold of the hem and lift the frock over her head. The telephone rang.

'Ignore the beastly thing,' she said.

'But it could be the police, checking.'

'Damn you for being so careful!' She kissed him to show her words had been spoken in love, not resentment. She went round the bed and sat by the side of the bedside table, lifted the receiver. She listened, spoke briefly, covered the mouthpiece. 'It's Hannah, which means this is going to be a half-hour call. Serves you right.'

She continued to listen far more than she spoke, saw he was looking at her and raised her gaze to the ceiling. Then she grinned and slipped the right-hand petticoat strap over her shoulder, transferred the receiver to her other ear, slid off the left-hand strap. She reached round her back to unclip her brassière, but held her right forearm against her breasts so that it did not drop away.

'As an act, it's old hat,' he said. 'But there could be some potential.'

'If you can't say better than that, you're not going to discover if there is . . .' She uncovered the mouthpiece. 'Yes, Hannah, I'm still here and I agree that Bill did seem to be unkind to you but, you know, he does have an odd sense of humour. The other day . . .' She stopped, waited, replaced the receiver. 'Cut off. So who's complaining?' She moved her right forearm, but the bra remained in place. 'How's that for technique?'

Instead of replying in the same vein, he took no notice of her and stared at the telephone. Then he moved past her and picked up the receiver, put it to his ear.

'Do feel free to observe priorities and phone your stock-broker,' she said.

'The line's dead.'

'We were cut off. I was delighted, but obviously you're in no hurry. Maybe you'd rather sleep in one of the other rooms?'

'There's no dialling tone.'

'Fascinating!'

'Can't you see, it may mean the wires have been cut?'

'Oh my God!' she whispered.

He raced out of the bedroom into the next one, shut the door to cut out any light from the landing, crossed to the single window. It was a clear night, but there was no moon and visibility was only somewhere between poor and moderate. He could just make out the bulks of the Mercedes and Sierra by the garage, which provided a yardstick; judging by that, there was no other vehicle around. He visually searched the yard and the garden. No signs of movements. Perhaps only someone panicking badly would have raised the fear that the interrupted call could mean the telephone lines had been cut. Yet there had been that telephone call in the morning from, according to Mrs Amis, a foreigner who had carefully not given his name . . .

He thought he saw two shadows move, but when he tried to concentrate his vision, there was nothing. Fear raised phantoms. But Agosto Seis must be desperate to keep the truth hidden and Herrero had proved himself to be a fanatic, willing to take any risk. Better a fool than a corpse. So accept that there were two men out there. They would be armed, probably with guns. For defence, he had nothing; not even a .410 shotgun. Then once they'd broken into the house, Kate and he would be helpless. They'd certainly kill him. They'd probably kill Kate because a dead witness wasn't dangerous; but before they killed her, they might . . .

No matter how futile his actions, he had to do something. Attack was said to be the best defence. But how did an unarmed man set about attacking two who were armed? In judo, one was taught to rely on the opponent's weakness, not on one's own strength. Jason had blackmailed him by playing on the most common of weaknesses . . . The men outside would surely reconnoitre the house before they broke in and therefore if he could use the same weakness that Jason had, in order to win the time and space to surprise them . . .

He raced back to the end bedroom. 'Come on downstairs.'

She was scared, but managing to control her fright. 'Is there someone out there?'

'There could be.'

'Then surely we'd be safer up here?'

'Not from the moment they got inside. We have to do something to hold their attention.'

'What's the good of that?'

He grabbed her hand and pulled her up from the bed; the bra fell away. 'Get your clothes back on.'

She dressed quickly, not understanding what he intended, but accepting that their only chance of survival— if, indeed, they were threatened—lay in carrying out whatever plan he had.

'Downstairs to the sitting-room, but don't put the hall light on.'

They made their way down the stairs and into the sitting-room. He switched on one of the standard lamps, went over to the window and drew the curtains until there was a gap between them of about six inches.

'They'll be able to see us . . .' she began.

He turned. 'On to the settee.'

He sat by her side and began to undo the buttons down the front of her frock. 'What are you doing?' she demanded, her voice high.

'Love, we've one chance. To get them so wrapped up in what they're watching and so excited by what they think they'll be watching in a minute or two that they temporarily put on hold what they've come to do.'

'But what then?'

'Once they're hooked, you'll have to entertain them on your own for a bit.'

She understood what he intended to do. 'Suppose . . .' she began fearfully. She stopped. If he were right and there were men out there, only this desperate move offered them any chance of survival.

He pulled her frock up and over her head, slipped her petticoat down, unclipped the brassière. After removing that, he began to fondle her nipples.

'Can you see anyone?' she whispered.

'If I'm half as passionate as I'm trying to make out, the last thing I'll be concerned with is who's out there.' He pulled her petticoat right down and off, ran his lips along her body; suddenly he stopped, as if something were troubling him, gesticulated: 'Keep 'em panting.'

He stood, hurried over to the door, went out. He hoped that any voyeurs would by now be so lasciviously excited that they wouldn't stop to wonder too deeply why he'd left off love-making at such a moment.

He went through the hall to the downstairs bathroom. There, he opened the window and scrambled over the sill to land on a small, semi-circular flowerbed in which grew plants that liked shade. On the far side of this was a brick-built extension which housed the boiler. He opened the door, very carefully because the hinges were quick to squeak. The present boiler was oil-fired, but at some time in the past there had obviously been a solid fuel one because a clinker rake lay propped up against the back wall, a welcome tribute to the it-may-come-in-handy-sometime syndrome. He reached round the boiler to get hold of this.

He took a firmer grip on the rake, stepped out of the boiler room and then walked on the grass. He came level with the end of the house. Keeping within its cover, he looked round the corner. With a sense of shock, made no less because it was expected, he saw that he had been right.

In the light which spilled out from the sitting-room, there were two men, their faces obscured by some form of covering.

He did not immediately move. There could be more intruders who'd not yet been drawn to the peepshow; or even one who was not an eager voyeur. The only way of finding out was to wait to discover if anyone else appeared; but the longer he waited before moving, the longer he gave the two men visible the opportunity to wonder why anyone enjoying so torrid a love scene should absent himself for any but the briefest of moments.

He stepped round the corner, tension making him all too conscious of the light rustle of clothing, the pad of shoes on grass, and the rush of breathing. But the two men remained facing the window, their attention caught by what they saw inside.

When within range, he raised the rake to shoulder height. Either he made more noise than before, or instinct alerted the nearer man, who began to turn. He shouted violently and the sudden blast of noise shocked both men into momentary immobility. He swung the rake, with shallow prongs pointing outwards, into the face of the nearer intruder, then kicked him in the crutch. The man screamed as he collapsed to the ground. Weston came forward, rake once more raised, and the toe of his right shoe became hooked on something and momentum sent him crashing to the ground.

He began to come to his feet, saw in the light of the sitting-room that the second man was pulling a gun free. There was no hope of closing before a shot was fired, but he was damned if he was going to wait for the inevitable and threw himself forward. His left hand hit something hard; as the pain shot up his fingers, he identified it as one of the rocks which bordered the flowerbed and this told him what it was that had earlier brought him crashing down.

Wrong bloody magic, he thought bitterly, remembering Kate's description of them. Then he realized that even if the rocks were not possessed of welcome magical qualities, this one was of a handy size. He transferred the rake to his aching left hand, took hold of the rock by a spiky, triangular outcrop, and came to his feet.

The gunman fired. The shot missed. He took aim more carefully, using both hands, convinced his target was helpless. Weston threw the rock, hoping that his schooldays' prowess as a mid-wicket fielder had not deserted him. It hadn't. The rock struck the gunman in the face a fraction of a second before he pulled the trigger. Again, the shot missed. Weston raced in, transferring the rake to his right hand as he did so, slammed the rake into the already damaged face. The gunman made a bubbling sound and clawed at his face with both hands, careless of what happened to the automatic, which fell. Weston picked it up, very conscious of the fact that not only was he uncertain how this one handled, he'd never fired any sort of a handgun.

He swung round. The first man was on his knees and clearly trying to pull something from his coat pocket. Weston raced over and used his shoe with vicious efficiency. The man collapsed and a spasmodic movement of his hand jerked out a gun. Weston kicked it clear, then picked it up. Two-gun Gary, he thought, as he began to tremble from reaction.

In the sitting-room, Kate was staring out, her face stretched with terror. He shouted that he was all right because one of her magical rocks had miraculously saved him.

CHAPTER 25

As were most estate agents, Fremlin was optimistic when it came to buying, very pessimistic when it came to selling; 'It's a nice situation, of course, but there is quite a lot of trouble at the moment with placing a house of this size.'

'Let's try it on the market and see what happens,' Weston said.

'Then I'd suggest extra publicity.'

Weston's immediate and unqualified assent cheered Fremlin up so much that he rashly opined that perhaps Francavilla might not be too difficult to sell, considering the asking price was a reasonable one.

Ten minutes later Weston watched Fremlin drive off, then he returned to the sitting-room where he poured himself another gin and tonic. The previous night Kate had asked if he was quite certain that he wanted to sell the house. His reply that he was, without any further qualification or explanation, had seemed to bother her. He guessed that her question had not been as straightforward as she had tried to make out. She wasn't yet certain that he suffered no deeper emotion over Stephanie's death than sad, compassionate regret and was scared that a part of his emotions might still belong to Stephanie. Time would convince her that it did not.

The front doorbell rang to interrupt his thoughts. His caller was Detective-Sergeant Waters.

'I thought I ought to have a quick word with you, Mr Weston. Hope it's not too inconvenient?'

Weston led the way back into the sitting-room and offered a drink. Waters said that since strictly speaking he wasn't on duty, he'd have a whisky and soda, thank you very much.

'What's brought you here this time?'

'To tell you that we ran an identity parade and Mrs Ackroyd picked out Herrero immediately, despite the battered face, and the second man, Coll, after a long hesitation. Her first identification will stand, her second, like as not, will be badly shaken in court. Though I could be wrong there because she's obviously pretty strong-minded, if a bit vague at times ... We've checked with Iberia and the two men, using the same false names on the passports they were carrying, flew into Heathrow on the Monday before your wife's death and back to Seville on the Thursday. Inquiries among the car hire firms working from the airport produced a week's rent of an Escort, light grey, by Herrero which was turned in before the end of the seven days; he's clearly remembered because he didn't make any fuss over the fact that, not having given them forty-eight hours' notice, there wouldn't be any refund. We questioned likely people around the common and tube station and found a newsvendor who's identified a photo of Herrero. He says Herrero stopped in a car and asked where Trefoil Road was. He remembers this because the man was a foreigner and didn't have the grace to buy a paper from him as thanks.

'We sent a request through to the Spanish authorities for information and their preliminary report came this morning. Herrero was not on duty during the relevant days. His wife says he was ill in bed. His girlfriend says that on the Friday he presented her with a cashmere twin set in a Heathrow duty-free shop carrier bag. We're trying to establish the date on which the twin set was bought.

'More directly in your interests, we've put all the facts before the Spanish police at top level and asked if they still wish to proceed with their application for your extradition on a charge of drug-smuggling. When they are convinced that this was a trumped-up charge, made at the instigation of a member of the force sufficiently high up to make certain it was processed, they'll undoubtedly withdraw it.'

'If they do, where will that leave me?'

Waters drank. 'Assuming the third man on the *Cristina* was Spanish, as we know for certain the first two were, there could be nothing illegal about them landing in Spain; therefore you can't be held guilty of an attempt to aid their illegal entry.'

'And the death of my wife?'

'Herrero and Coll will almost certainly either be charged with her murder or, less likely, her manslaughter. While I can't officially confirm that you are no longer under any suspicion, unofficially I can say that that's the case . . . You can forget all your worries.' He raised his glass and emptied it.

Weston cleared his throat. 'That still leaves one question, doesn't it?'

'Does it?'

'When I had to persuade you that Mrs Stevens desperately needed help, the only way I could manage was to admit I'd travelled to Spain on a false passport.'

'You admitted this to whom?'

'I've just said—to you.'

Waters pursed his lips. 'Can't say I can remember anything of the sort. You must be mixing me up with someone else.' He put the glass down on a table, stood. 'I'd better be moving on.'

Weston hesitated, then said as he stood: 'I'd like to say thanks, but maybe in the circumstances that wouldn't be appropriate?'

'Can't say, really.' He walked towards the door, said over his shoulder: 'I hope the information's of no future consequence to you, but just for the record, two thousand for a passport is a real steal. The going rate is around seven hundred and fifty, or five hundred for a trashy EEC one.'

Weston parked in front of the garage, picked up the parcel from the front passenger seat, walked down the drive and around the house. As he approached the front door, Kate opened it. She studied him. 'You look like a cat that's just found a whole pint of cream.'

'Make that a gallon . . . I was about to drive down when Detective-Sergeant Waters called. He's told me I'm in the clear, both over Stephanie's death and the trip in the *Cristina*.'

'No more nightmares? Oh my God, I can't believe it.'

'Will this help convince you.' He handed her the parcel.

She unwrapped it to disclose an elaborately fashioned black and gold container on which was embossed, in flowing script, Bejoule's *Le Rêve*.